DECEMBER FORTY-FOUR

Jack Dunn

Commonwealth Books Inc.,

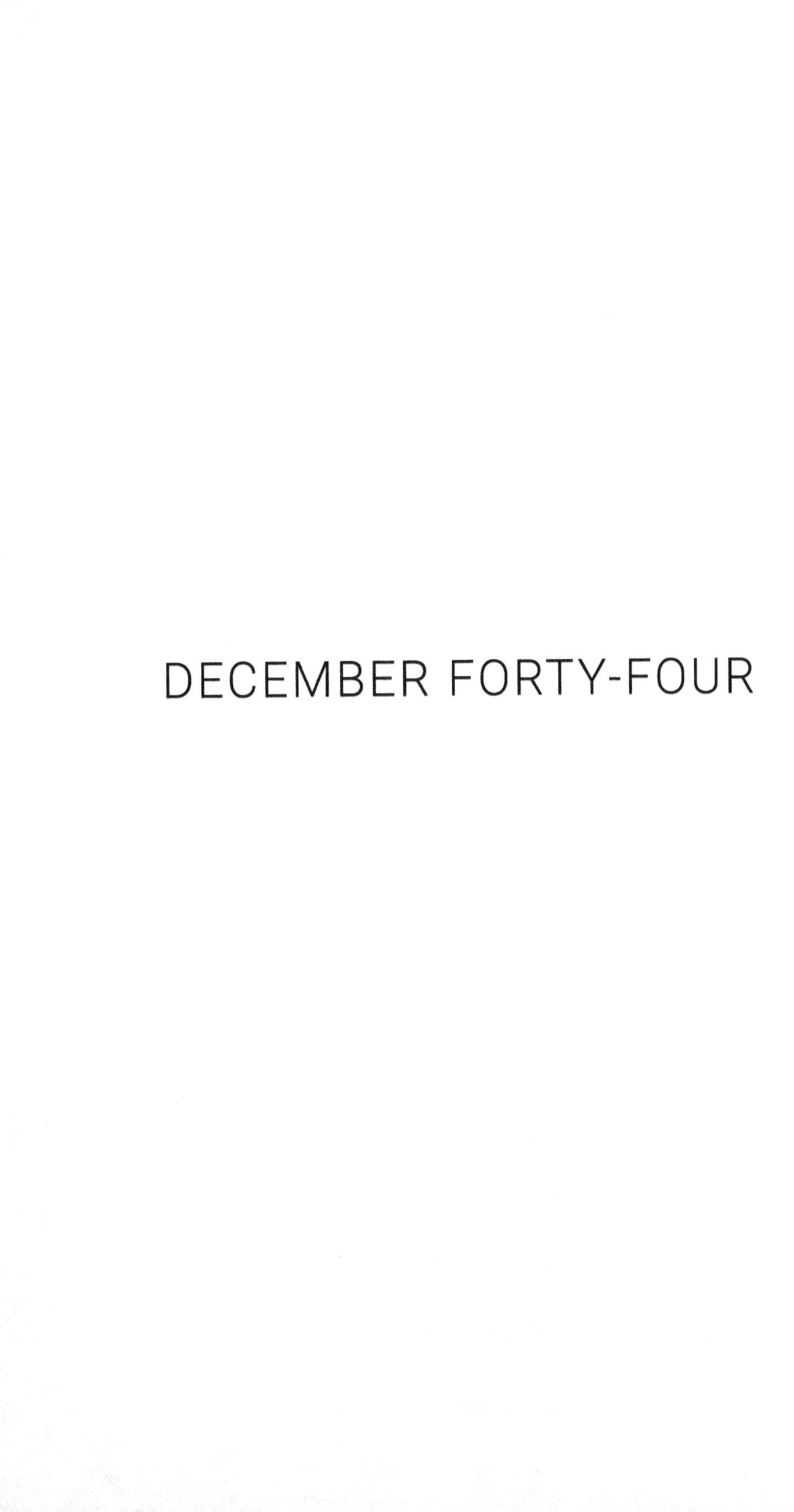

DECEMBER FORTY-FOUR

A Commonwealth Publications Trade
DECEMBER FORTY-FOUR
This edition published 2022
 by Commonwealth Books Inc.,
All rights reserved

Library of Congress Control Number: 2022933832

ISBN: 978-1-892986-41-5 (Trade)
ISBN: 978-1-892986-41-2(E-PUB)

This work is a novel and any similarity to actual persons or events is purely
coincidental.

First Commonwealth Books Trade Edition: June 2022

PUBLISHED BY COMMONWEALTH BOOKS, INC.,
www.commonwealthbooks@aol.com
www.commonwealthbooksinc.com

Manufactured in the United States of America

For my parents, Reed and Marjorie Dunn.

PREFACE

The summer and early fall of 1944 were full of hope. The Second Front spread out from Normandy after D Day into France and the low countries, with the enemy continually pushed back. Pundits spoke of the war in Europe being over by year's end. Wives and mothers prayed their citizen soldiers would return home for Christmas, and everyone hoped for an early end to rationing of gasoline, food, and other restricted items. Military successes continued unto early fall, and the borders of the enemy's homeland were tantalizingly close.

For one family on the Home Front, fall seemed very abbreviated. By late November, early signs of winter appeared. An early snowfall replaced the classical Thanksgiving landscape of autumn leaves, pumpkins, and corn shocks in the field. In retrospect, it might have been a harbinger of the coming holiday season, perhaps an interlude to offer sharp contrast to happier times, remembered only by adults before the distress and woe of the Great Depression and the shortage and human anguish brought on by the war.

The ever-present anxiety the hostilities engendered was somewhat mitigated by the possibility of an early end to the conflict. Those hopes were shattered by a major enemy counteroffensive in mid-December that would later become known as the Battle of the Bulge. The event thwarted the Allies' expectations for an early victory and resulted in a pall over the Yuletide season. The family was forced to improvise, as they struggled against forces beyond their control to mold a holiday experience that would be within acceptable expectations, if not memorable.

One

When he heard the door to the living room open, Sam Minor looked up from the kitchen table to see his wife, Clara, entering the room.

He sipped from his coffee. "Kinda early for you to be up, isn't it?"

"Yes, it is, but I woke up and was cold and couldn't go back to sleep."

"It's almost frigid in this old farmhouse. I had one of the Pittsburgh radio stations on earlier, and they said a cold front moving down from the Great lakes into western Pennsylvania brought a little light snow with it. Here we are, only a day after Thanksgiving, but it feels like January."

"Did you hear any war news?"

He nodded. "Things seem pretty quiet in western Europe. The commentator offered the opinion that the Allies were taking a breather to get resupplied and bring up reinforcements. They might not start the push out of France and into Germany until after the first of the year."

Clara, lighting a cigarette, walked to the kitchen stove.

"There's only a dribble of coffee left. I'll start a new pot." She paused. "What's on your schedule for today?"

"With this change in the weather and maybe more snow coming, I'd better see about bringing the beef cattle in from the other side of the farm to those shelters out back of the barn. They'll be easier to feed out there and will have some protection from the weather.

"I'll be out at the barn, milking for an hour and a half, so I'd like you to get the boys up in a little while. I'll need their help with the beef cattle."

"OK, Sam. You sure that's not too much for a ten-year-old?"

"Jimmie will be all right. It shouldn't be anything strenuous. We'll just be walking at a normal pace, and the cattle will follow. Reed will have the tough job at the back end to keep stragglers moving. At sixteen, he's almost as big as me, so he'll be fine."

When Jimmie woke, his first sensation was that his exposed arm was really cold and uncomfortable. *Wow! No wonder!* He pulled the arm back under the comforter and rubbed it briskly. *The room's really cold.*

He turned his head to look out the window. *It's already light out. I'd guess it's about the time we'd usually get up for school. Holy cow! Look at the little skim of snow on the floor under the window. No wonder it's cold. It must've snowed last night, and some seeped in, but at least it's warm here under the covers. Glad we don't have school today.*

He was surprised to hear the door open at the bottom of the back stairs from the dining room.

"Reed! Jimmie!" his mother called. "Time to get up! Breakfast is ready!"

After a brief pause, she added a bit louder, "Boys, it's time to get up."

"Aw, Mom," Reed said from across the room. "There's no school today. Couldn't we lay in for a while?"

"Afraid not. Your dad needs both of you. We had a little snow overnight, and he's pretty sure there's more on the way. He wants the beef cattle brought over from the far side of the farm to the shelter behind the barn."

"OK, Mom. We'll get moving."

The older boy pushed back the covers and sat up on the edge of the bed. He retrieved clothing from a nearby chair and his shoes from the floor and walked out of the room.

"You might as well stay under and keep warm while I get my things on in the bathroom," Reed said. "Then it's your turn, Squirt."

Jimmie didn't reply, glad for the extra minutes of warmth under the mound of covers, but the respite was brief. Reed returned shortly to gather a small pile of clothes from the wicker stool near the closet opening and walked back out.

"OK, Jimmie. I'll take your stuff to the bathroom. You can make the mad dash when you're ready, but don't take too long. Dad's probably in a pucker to get the beef cattle over here."

Half an hour later, the brothers were downstairs in the kitchen, eating breakfast of buckwheat pancakes and ham slices. Clara stood by the kitchen range with a cup of coffee in one hand and a cigarette in the other.

In her early forties, she was an attractive woman. She had a pretty face and slender build, though one of her brothers-in-law embarrassed her at a family dinner by remarking she had the best-muscled legs of any woman he ever saw. It might have been her nature to be trim, but the Great Depression's twelve-hour workdays for a farm wife didn't lend themselves to weight gain. Jimmie knew only her gentle nature, ready smile, and happy attitude. He was vaguely aware she had a college education and had briefly worked as a school teacher before marrying.

Because of their ages, Jimmie and Reed weren't even aware of the family's abrupt, unexpected change from a comfortable lifestyle to one that was barely above subsistence following the stock market crash of 1929. Basic necessities were met, and the parents shielded the boys from fantasizing about more-affluent times.

"Don't gobble your food so fast," Clara said, "or you'll have a bellyache if you have to chase any of those cows. Your dad won't worry about a couple minutes' delay one way or the other."

Before either of the boys could reply, the outside door opened, and Sam stepped in from the cold. "Any more coffee, Clara? I could use a warm-up."

Without an answer, she took a cup down from the cupboard, filled it from the pot on the stove, and placed it at Sam's customary spot at the head of the table.

Only two years older than Clara, Sam was just a bit over six-feet tall, muscular, and not overweight. His dark hair had only a few strands of gray, and by most standards, he was considered handsome. There was a quickness about him, only occasionally marred by a bit of stiffness and an occasional grimace when arising from a sitting position that was the result of a football injury as a young man.

Reed and Jimmie were somewhat in awe of their father, a take-charge man who, in their eyes, always had a solution to life's problems. He was easygoing but could be stern if need be. At that stage in their lives, neither of the boys questioned his authority as the family patriarch.

"That coffee hits the spot," Sam said. "Are you boys up for a little cattle drive this morning?"

With his mouth full of food, Jimmie nodded.

"Yeah, we're ready, Dad," Reed said. "Think we'll have any trouble?"

"I don't think so. Those animals have more sense than people give them credit for. Most were over here last winter, so they'll remember the shelter. I think they can sense the change in the weather and will be glad for safe haven until spring."

Sam paused for a moment. "First, we'll go by the cattle pens, and I'll call 'em down from the hollow at the edge of the woods where they usually gather to stay out of the wind or rain or snow. We'll open the big gate and start them through and across the bottom. I'll have the salt bag with me, and I'll drop some for them. That'll keep them coming. The main thing is to let them go at their own pace and not get excited. Don't yell or run, or, before you know it, we'll have cows scattered all over hell's half acre.

"Clara, I'll need you to help out again like last year. Keep an eye out. When you hear us coming up the bottom, come stand in the road so they'll know to go up the lane and out to the barn."

"I can do that, Sam," she replied. "In the meantime, I'll take care of the dishes. I suspect Marge will come down for breakfast and coffee any time now. You boys listen to your dad and do what he says so you get the job done. Reed, look after your brother."

A short time later, Sam and the boys left the house and started out. The fact that it wasn't one of the boys' ordinary chores and held the possibility of some excitement made it something to look forward to.

Jimmie was pleased to have a part in moving the cattle. *Lots of times I don't get to help. They either think I'm too little, or they're afraid I'll get hurt around the tractor or something. I know I can do this. It's pretty cold, though.*

The trio walked down the slope from the house and across the footbridge over the small stream, across the flat bottom land toward the cattle pens.

"The old backstop for the baseball field looks ready to fall apart," Reed said.

"Yeah, it looks pretty bad," Sam remarked. "There hasn't been a team playing here for five years. I guess there's nobody to take care of it."

"Why is that?"

"Fellows my age are too old to play, some of the young guys left the area looking for jobs, and then the war came. Others joined up or were drafted. There aren't enough left to field a team."

"So is that the end of baseball around here?"

"Maybe, maybe not. If the war is over in the next year or so, and the men come back, it might start up again. We'll have to wait and see."

Beyond the abandoned baseball field, they walked under a railroad trestle.

"The work crew for the railroad isn't around today," Reed observed. "I wonder why."

"Maybe they got an extra day off to go with Thanksgiving," Sam said. "I don't doubt they deserve it. They been working those fellows pretty hard, ten- and twelve-hour days. It's just as well they aren't here while we're trying to move the cattle. They usually have a fire built, and there's some commotion goin' on. The cows aren't around people much, and it doesn't take much to spook them."

"Dad, what are they doing with the trestle and the railroad?" Jimmie asked.

"They're widening the rails to standard gauge, and it looks like they're trying to strengthen the trestle with newer, stronger beams."

"What's standard gauge?"

"Gauge is the distance between the rails. When they built this railroad.... Let's see. It was back when your grandfather was about your age. They built it using what they call narrow gauge. The distance between the rails is several inches less than standard, which is now common with most railroads."

"Why are they going to all this work to change it?"

"I guess some government big shots decided it was part of the war effort."

"I still don't understand."

"I heard it has to do with coal. Coal is necessary for making steel and other things that are important for our soldiers and sailors— boats, tanks, guns. There's a lot of coal under the ground here, and they might need it to make more things depending on how long the war lasts."

"Why don't we dig up the coal ourselves?" Reed asked. "We could sell it and get rich."

Sam chuckled. "There are two reasons. First, coal is really deep in the ground. It takes lots of money, which we don't have, to hire the workers and buy the equipment to get it out of the ground. Besides, the coal doesn't belong to us. The big coal companies bought the rights to mine the coal years ago from your grandfather."

Past the trestle, they continued toward the cattle pasture. Jimmie had to exert himself to keep up with his brother and father, but that kept him warm. *I'm glad we don't have much snow on the ground. I probably couldn't keep up if I was wading through snow.*

Looking beyond the cattle pens, he saw the big hickory trees on the far side of the small stream that flowed through the field.

We got a lot of nuts from them last month, he realized. *Hickory nut cake is my favorite. Maybe Mom will make one for Christmas dinner.*

His private thoughts were interrupted when they reached the gate by the cattle pens.

"OK, Boys," Sam said. "Now the fun begins. I'll open this gate and start calling the cows. Both of you stand off to one side. When I get them down here, I'll try to lead them through the gate. Jimmie, I want you to come with me. Reed, you bring up the rear and keep stragglers from straying to the side. Both of you remember what I said. No yelling or running. Keep them calm, but try to keep them moving."

Sam walked ahead. He went only a short distance before he called to the cattle.

He sure has a strong voice, Jimmie thought. *It doesn't sound like the noises cows make, but it must be close, because it usually brings them down. Sure enough! Here they come.*

The wind blew snow around, leaving a few places bare. As the cattle neared, Sam dropped small handfuls of salt onto the ground. The animals, recognizing what he did, hurried to lick up the treat they relished. Sam reversed direction. As he dropped more handfuls of salt, the cattle followed just as Sam predicted.

Sam nodded to Jimmie. "OK, Son. I counted thirty-two. That's all of them. Let's walk at a slow pace through the gate and down through the bottom field."

The cattle followed Sam. A few minutes later, the herd traversed the bottom field, crossed the stream, and started up the moderate grade toward the farmstead.

"Now, Jimmie, we need to speed up a bit without running. Go up through the gate and then turn left and stand in the road, so the cattle know to go straight up the lane. Your mom's already there, standing in the road to the right."

Jimmie did as directed, and the process was brought to a successful conclusion. A short while later, the family stood at the rear of the barn, watching the cattle in and around the shelters. Some of the cows lay down as if resting, while others fed on the hay in the racks adjacent to the shelters. A few calves ran around, playfully butting each other.

"I'm glad that's over," Sam said. "They seem pretty content. Now I don't have to worry about losing any of them when the weather turns bad. The *Farmer's Almanac* says it'll be a harsh winter."

"Anything in the herd that'll find its way onto the table?" Clara asked.

He smiled. "I wouldn't be surprised. There's a couple yearling steers in there. In a day or so, after they're settled, I'll cut one of them out and put him in that side pen and start graining him. A few weeks into the new year, he'll be ready to butcher. That's a pretty good deal, since we don't have to use ration stamps for our own meat. It was a good thing we got that frozen food locker in town the spring after Pearl Harbor. That's where he'll end up."

"That sounds good to me. I don't know about you men folk, but I'm getting cold. Anyone else heading back to the house with me?"

"Well, it's a bit chilly," Sam admitted. "I hope it lasts until next weekend, though. I'd like to get the hog butchering done. I wouldn't mind getting warmed up, but I need to get the tractor to the store and put gas in it, unless.... Reed, you want to do that chore?"

"Sure, Dad. I'll do that."

"Not much of a surprise there," Clara said, smiling. "He'd jump at the chance to drive the tractor even if it was twenty below. Come with me, Jimmie. I know you're cold. How does hot chocolate sound?"

"Sounds good to me.

When Jimmie and Clara entered the kitchen, she looked around with a puzzled expression.

Marge should've been down here by now, she thought. *Damn. Every time she comes, she finds a way to make me feel like a hired girl. Sure, she grew up here, but that doesn't give her the right to act like Miss Priss. Oh, well. She'll never change. No use wishing.*

Clara, walking into the living room, called up the stairwell, "Marge? Are you OK up there?"

After a brief pause, they heard footsteps in the upstairs hall.

"I'm OK, Clara. I haven't croaked yet. I'm trying to correct the tests I gave last week. From some of the results, I'm beginning to think I should have taken up a different profession. I'll be down in a few minutes to help with lunch."

When Clara returned to the kitchen, Jimmie had a question for her.

"Why does Aunt Marge called dinner lunch?"

"It's the difference between farmers and city folk. Farmers have a long workday. By the middle of the day, they're ready for a big meal to have the energy to work all afternoon, so we have two cooked meals. City folk have a shorter day and eat a light meal at midday. Even the factory men carry a lunch bucket with sandwiches and such, just like you carry to school. That's the best answer I have."

Sometime later, Jimmie and his parents enjoyed the warmth of the kitchen when they heard the tractor returning up the lane. A few minutes later, Reed came inside.

"Anything going on at the store?" Clara asked.

"No. Just the usual bunch. They had the mail sorted, so I brought that back."

"Let's see what we got. We'll be getting Christmas cards soon. How about this? Jimmie, you have a letter. It's a V mail from your cousin, Rex. Here you go."

Jimmie eagerly opened it. "Boy, this is hard to read."

"That's because it's photographed to half the original size, and Rex's penmanship was never that great to start with."

"I don't understand." Jimmie frowned. "Why don't they just send the letter instead of taking a picture of it?"

"It's a matter of space and money," Sam answered. "One letter doesn't seem like much, but there's thousands, probably even millions, of letters going back and forth between fellows in the service overseas and their families and friends back home. That's tons of letters. They take up a lot of space in planes and ships. If we can reduce the space they take up, they can use it for bullets, supplies, and food the fellows need. Does that make sense?"

"I guess so."

"Now that's been settled, will you share the letter with us?"

"OK. Let's see."

Dear Jimmie,

How are you doing? I'm doing OK and haven't been sick or anything. The fall weather around where I am has been OK. The leafs here have turned, but they aren't as nice as at home. I'm not allowed to tell where I'm at or what I'm doing.

I did get leave a couple weeks back and some of us went to Paris. French girls are pretty. Ha. Ha. I guess by the time you get this, you'll be thinking about Christmas. What do you want?

Guess that's about all. Say hello to your mom and dad and big brother for me. Be a good boy.

Your Cousin,

Rex

"That was a real nice letter," Clara said. "You'll have to write back soon."

"I guess, but you'll have to help me. I won't know what to say."

"I'm getting hungry," Reed said. "What's for dinner, Mom?"

"We've got lots of leftovers from Thanksgiving. How would a hot turkey sandwich and some stuffing on the side sound to you? There's pumpkin pie left for dessert."

"Sounds great to me. Come on, Jimmie. We'd better get washed up."

The boys barely left the kitchen when Marge appeared. "Did I time it so I missed out on all the work?"

"No," Clara replied. "We'll find something for you to do. This meal won't require a lot of effort, since we're eating light." She repeated what she described to Reed.

"That'll be fine. At least I can set the table. It looks like someone brought over the mail from the post office. Anything interesting?"

"There's big excitement over a V mail Jimmie got from Rex."

"That's nice. Couldn't have been a world of information in it, I wouldn't think. I write to all my nephews who're in the service on a regular basis, and I hear back, but they're restricted in what they can write. All we know is that he's somewhere going up against the Germans, probably in France. From what I see in the paper, we're doing pretty well."

"It seems that way," Sam said. "I hope it continues."

"Any reason to think it won't?"

"I was reading a column the other day. A so-called expert said the Allies were getting close to the German border in a lot of areas. In a couple places, they've crossed it. He seemed to think when the Germans are backed up to defending their homeland, their resistance will stiffen."

"I hope he's wrong."

"So do I."

The boys returned to the kitchen.

"We ready to eat now, Mom?" Reed asked.

"Good Lord, Boy, you'd think you were starving. It'll be a few minutes yet. Jimmie, I have a job for you."

"What's that?"

"I haven't had time to mix the coloring into the margarine. I put it out in that mixing bowl after breakfast, so it should be soft enough to stir. The little packet of powder's beside it. You know what to do. We'll be ready to eat by the time you're finished."

In a few minutes, the family sat at the dining room table.

"You know, Clara," Marge said, "I enjoy Thanksgiving leftovers as much as the big feast. Sometimes, it seems like the flavors get more intense."

"That's probably true, but it could also be that we only have these things a couple times a year. We associate them with the holidays and having family members around. Those are happy times."

Clara paused. "Sam, I was thinking after you mentioned Reed being at the store how things are probably so different now than when we were young. We had passenger train service to Washington and Waynesburg, as well as points in between, which created more activity. We also had regular freight service until 1938. Not much left now, is there?"

"No. The little dinky shows up once every two weeks or so. It might have a roll of fence or some big bags of fertilizer, but a lot of times there's nothing. I heard that the right-of-way agreements with the property owners require them to provide a minimum level of service, so that's what the dinky is for."

"It made all the difference in the world to a lot of people. We probably wouldn't have been able to go to high school, if we hadn't been able to use the train to get into Washington."

"The only option would have been to stay with Dad's brother's family there."

"Ugh."

"By the way, Marge, I just remembered that someone you'll recall from days gone by showed up at the station a couple months ago."

"Who was that?"

"Arch Yeager."

"Oh, for pity's sake! I haven't thought about him in years. He was a few years older than me but quite a guy—very handsome. All the young women thought he was the cream of the crop."

Reed laughed. "Handsome? Are you kidding? That old geezer?"

Marge looked at Sam with a questioning expression.

"Marge," Sam said, "you wouldn't recognize him. The years haven't been good to him, though from what I heard it was the hard life he lived with a lot of alcoholism. He weighs twice what he once did, and he must have arthritis pretty bad. He's lost some teeth and most of his hair, and he walks with great difficulty. I'd say he looks twenty years older than his actual age."

"Well, that's a surprise. There were some unusual circumstances with his leaving the area back in the teens, weren't there?"

Sam grinned. "That's one way to describe it. Self-preservation is another. He was quite a ladies' man and got involved with a married woman up by West Union. The husband found out, and he came after Arch with a twelve gauge, but he got away. His lady friend and her husband left the area for good, but it was thirty years before Arch came back."

"Where'd he go? What did he do all those years?"

"I never spoke to him,, but I've heard he was in the Youngstown area working on the railroad. What he actually did, I don't know."

"What's he doing now?"

"He spends his days at the store. Frank gives him a little money for watching the store when he's away or when he's in back to sort mail. He gets a small pension from the railroad. That buys enough food and beer for him to get falling-down drunk a couple times a month."

"Where does he live?"

"Just up the road past the store at the Dunn place. They let him fix up an old outbuilding. I don't recall what it used to be, probably a corn crib or chicken house. I believe he has an old wood-burning cook stove, a bed, a table, and chair. That serves his needs."

"My, oh my. That's quite a story. It's sad to think how the personable young man ended up so poorly."

Two

It was Sunday morning, and breakfast was long over. Reed and Jimmie, dressed for Sunday school, waited for their customary ride.

Reed looked out the front window. "I don't see them coming yet, but it shouldn't be very long. Better get your boots on. We don't want to hold 'em up."

"I'm hurrying the best I can. I'm having trouble with this knot in my shoelace. There. I got it."

Clara walked into the living room. "You boys both have something to put on the collection plate?"

They nodded.

"Didn't I hear you coughing upstairs when you were dressing, Jimmie? I hope you aren't coming down with something again. Is your throat sore?"

"Not really. Maybe a little scratchy."

"Maybe you should take a nap after we get home from church and dinner's over. You dad and I will be along later for the church service. I see you have your Junior Commando sweat shirt, Jimmie. How about you, Reed? Where's yours?"

Reed was thoughtful for a few seconds. "I think that's kind of kid's stuff. I don't mean collecting scrap and other stuff we do. That's important, but I don't have to wear pretend military stuff to do that. Dan Bristor and I were talking about that the other day, and we're the only two in the group who are sixteen. It makes us feel silly."

Clara agreed with him but wanted to respond carefully to avoid changing Jimmie's mind about the organization. "You're old enough to make your own decisions about your clothing. Incidentally, will there be something special with your group?"

"I think so," Reed said. "Sunday school will let out early, and there'll be something in front of the church. I heard some kids who collected the most milkweed pods will get a ribbon or a medal."

"That'll be nice. You boys got several bags of those. Maybe you'll be among the lucky ones."

Reed shrugged. "Maybe."

"What's anybody want with those milkweed pods, anyway?" Jimmie asked.

"They explained that when they brought the bags around," Reed said, shaking his head in disgust. "If you'd just listen...."

"Don't be hard on your brother," Clara said. "It's part of the war effort, Jimmie. They'll be used to make life preservers for the servicemen. The stuff they used before the war came from somewhere in South America. It's called *kapok*. It's hard to get now, because it has to be shipped so far, and it's dangerous because of enemy submarines. They think the milkweed pods will float just as well as the *kapok* for life preservers."

A car horn interrupted the conversation.

"That's your ride with Frank and Ester," Clara said. "Hustle outside. Don't keep them waiting."

She thought it was very neighborly of Frank and Ester Hoge to take the boys to Sunday school each week, especially with gas rationing. Clara could have taken them and returned for Sam later. Sunday was the only day Sam didn't have to work, so taking a nap after the morning milking was welcome. For reasons Sam never explained, it was clear he had little respect for Milo Day, the adult men's class teacher at church.

Frank owned the country general store and was also the postmaster. He was the surviving heir of a family who owned considerable acreage for several generations. Selling the coal-mining rights yielded a substantial nest egg. Frank's regular income came from the proceeds of the general store and the salary for managing their small rural post office in the other half of the same building.

Clara smiled, thinking what an interesting couple Frank and Ester were. Physically, they were very different. Frank was shorter than average and very slender. Ester was two inches taller than Frank and was very stout, if not fat. Their personalities were dissimilar, too. Frank was soft-spoken and not prone to blunt opinions on issues or individuals. Ester was very outspoken concerning politics, race, religion, and the conduct of the war. She didn't hesitate to criticize the statements or opinions of others, especially Frank. True to his character, he never contradicted her ridicule and accepted it with a nod and smile.

The two-and-a-half-mile ride to church took only a few minutes, but Jimmie always looked forward to it. A different direction than going to school or town, it provided a change of scenery. Just beyond the old schoolhouse, they passed the oil company tool yard, with two small buildings sided in corrugated metal. He saw a pile of metal casings used for drilling wells.

As they drove on, Jimmie looked across the way at the railroad line on the opposite side of the valley. *You sure can see a lot more now that the leaves are off the trees,* he thought, *like that railroad line.*

"Look, Reed," he said. "There's the horseshoe curve."

"Yep. I don't guess it's goin' anywhere."

Ignoring his brother's sarcasm, Jimmie said, "Remember how Dad said in the old says, the fellows with the fastest riding horses tried to race the train going around the curve? Could they beat the train?"

"I don't know. Maybe if the train was going upgrade and going slower."

They soon turned off the main road, passing several houses in the village of West Union, until they reached their destination.

Frank parked in front of the church. "I'll be sure to be back by the time church is finished," he said, as Ester and the boys got out.

As the trio walked toward the church, Jimmie asked, "Why doesn't Frank ever stay for church?"

"It's always been a mystery to me," she replied tersely. "If you ever find out, let me know."

Once inside, the boys walked to the portion of the building where youth Sunday school activities were held. The opening activities consisted of singing *Onward Christian Soldiers* and a prayer led by an older girl prior to their Bible study. The young people were divided into three groups roughly similar to the way public schools were segmented. Reed was in the second section, while Jimmie was in the primary. A small room to one side contained a few toddlers.

Jimmie, anxious for Bible study to begin, rehearsed his memorized Bible verse for the day. Every Sunday beginning with that day, each of them had to memorize a Bible verse that began with each of the letters in his or her first name.

Once all the children were seated around the big table, Mrs. Hackney began their lesson. "Who'd like to go first with his verse?"

The youngsters all looked at each other, but no one volunteered.

"Oh, come on, now. Don't be bashful. How about you, Jimmie?"

Why'd she have to pick on me? he wondered. *Might as well get it over with.*

"OK." He stood. "Jesus said, 'I am the way, the truth, and the life.'"

"That's excellent, Jimmie. Can you tell the rest of the class what that means?"

"I guess it means we're supposed to live our lives like Jesus said we should."

"How would we do that?"

No one spoke for a few seconds, then Betty Carvin said, "Follow the Golden Rule."

"Good answer," Mrs. Hackney said, "but let's not forget the Ten Commandments. All right. Does anyone have a verse from the Old Testament?"

Only one hand went up.

"All right, Frank. What do you have for us?"

"This is from Deuteronomy. 'For the Lord your God is He that goeth with you to fight against your enemies.'"

"I think I know, Frank, but will you tell us why you chose that verse?"

He smiled. "Both my older brothers are in the Army. Pete is somewhere in Italy, and Charles is in the Philippines. I hope the Lord is looking after them."

"I'm sure we all share that hope with you. Before we continue, let's bow our heads and say a silent prayer that the Lord will look after Frank's brothers and all the other servicemen."

Following the prayer, the class proceeded with few diversions. Soon, the children reassembled with the other sections for the closing song and announcements, which included announcing the time for the Christmas program to be held on Wednesday evening before Christmas Day.

Shortly thereafter, they went outside and stood in a straight line. All but two wore their Junior Commando sweatshirts and over-seas caps. The Sunday School superintendent came out of the church and down the steps to stand before the youngsters.

She smiled. "I'm very proud of all of you. The number of bags of milkweed pods you collected was among the highest of all the groups that participated. More than that, medals have been awarded to each person who harvested ten or more bags. Three of you did just that. Harvey Ramsey, George Brand, and Reed Minor, please step forward to receive your medals. Congratulations!"

As the medals were handed out, the minister in his car drove up and parked. Reverend French left the vehicle and walked quickly over to the ceremony.

"I'm glad I got here in time to see the awards," he said. "I really had to push that old DeSoto to make it here from Rogersville." He paused. "It's gratifying that you young folks are doing your part for the war effort. Terrible things are happening in the world, and everything we can do to bring this awful war to an end is part of God's way. Now let's move inside and worship the Lord."

Reed sat with young people in his age bracket in the last row of seats. Jimmie sat with his parents, who arrived just as the others entered the church. He knew the service usually started around eleven o'clock and was over by noon, though there was no clock on the wall.

It always seems to go on for so long, he thought. *I wish I had a wristwatch so I'd know how much longer I'll have to sit here. He's been giving his sermon for several minutes, and there are only a couple more things on the program after that. It shouldn't be much longer.*

He was paying enough attention to the pastor's message that he knew the theme was about Thanksgiving and being thankful for God's blessings. He became more attentive when he noticed Reverend French enumerating how much more the congregation had in the way of food and warm shelter compared to the men in the service.

With his voice raised louder for emphasis, Reverend French said, "And we should be thankful that we are not, like them, in cold and muddy places, with the enemy shooting at us and causing grievous wounds or worse."

He paused to let the impact of his words be absorbed in the minds of his congregation. There was complete silence for a few seconds, then it was interrupted by quiet sobbing that grew into a piteous wail and cry for help.

"God.... Oh, my God!"

The congregation turned to see three forlorn individuals sitting near the rear of the sanctuary on the left. A middle-aged woman sat with head bowed while her body shook with emotion. To her left, a man of similar age put his arm around her and patted her shoulder for comfort. To her right, a distraught teenage girl with tears flowing down her cheeks held the woman's hand.

Clara whispered to Ester, who sat in front of her, "That's the Cox family. They got word a few days ago that their son, Michael, was killed in Italy."

Several parishioners turned toward the minister, as if asking him to deal with the situation. He quickly left the pulpit and walked back to the grieving family. From the row in front of them, he reached across the seats and took the woman's hands.

"Mildred, I know your sorrow is beyond words, and what I can say in the way of comfort seems trivial, but Michael was a fine, God-fearing young man. I believe he was doing God's work. We're just beginning to learn the extent of the atrocities our enemies have committed. Your family's sacrifice will help bring that to an end. Michael gave his life in a noble effort."

The grieving woman composed herself in a few minutes. Reverend French said a few more words to the family and returned to his pulpit to face the congregation.

"Friends, I'm somewhat drained of energy and emotion, and I'm not sure what else I could say this morning as a spiritual message. On page eighty-nine in your hymnals is my favorite Thanksgiving hymn, *Faith of Our Fathers*. Let us conclude our Sunday service with this as our closing prayer and song."

A somber group exited the church a few minutes later. Those who walked to the service from nearby homes left, while others got into their cars. The brief visiting and neighborly conversation that usually followed the service was abbreviated, seeming somehow inappropriate.

With Sam driving, the Minor family headed home. Their routine conversation after church was absent for most of the drive.

"Dad, what's those 'trocities Reverend French was talking about?" Jimmie asked.

Sam paused for a few seconds. "Jimmie, there's been talk that the Germans are locking people away in camps where they're all crowded together. They don't have enough food, clothing, or heat.

They're treated mean. Worse, some die. These aren't soldiers. They're civilians, ordinary men, women, and children."

"I don't think I've heard anything about that on the news, Sam," Clara said.

"There's been very little on the news, but something's going on. Our history teacher, Morris Kaplan, told me his people are getting the worst of it over there. He tells me the Jews have organizations with ways of getting information out. It's ugly."

"What's a Jew?" Jimmie asked.

"Jesus was a Jew," Clara said. "The Bible says the Jews are God's chosen people."

"I sure don't understand. If they're God's chosen, why does someone want to lock 'em up in a camp and be mean to them?"

"I don't have a good answer for you," Sam replied. "It seems like some folks think it makes them feel better to look down on other people just because of which church they go to or the color of their skin. Like I've said before, we don't live in a perfect world. If it was, we wouldn't be in a war."

He paused before continuing. "It's a shame about that Cox boy. He was a nice young fella and a hard worker. He was young, so he never had much of a chance to experience the good things in life."

"That's true," Clara said. "He graduated from high school last June."

Sam shook his head. "He was shipped overseas in September, wasn't he? You can't tell me he had enough training in just a couple months to know what he was doing. They're throwing those kids into it like cannon fodder. The family has nothing to show for it but a gold star in a window."

"What's a gold star for?" Jimmie asked. "Is it like a Christmas ornament?"

"I'm afraid not, Jimmie," Sam said. "I'm sure you've seen the little flags hanging in people's windows, mostly with blue stars on them. That means a family member is in the military. If the star is gold, it means he was killed.

"It's gonna be tough on that family. Harry and Mildred aren't much older than us, but he's not in good shape. It doesn't take much before he's all played out. If Allison and I hadn't helped him with the hay this summer, his cows would be eating snowballs this winter, and I know they were counting on Mike to take over."

There was no further conversation the rest of the way home.

When they returned and entered the house through the front door to the living room, Clara and Sam continued into the kitchen.

"Boys, you'd better go upstairs and change out of your Sunday clothes," Clara called. "We won't be eating for a while." She turned to Sam. "There's half a pot of coffee. I'll warm it up."

"Good. I could use some." He paused. "I didn't want to mention this in front of the boys, especially Jimmie, but Morris told me more about the war atrocities going on."

"What's that?"

"He had a small newspaper clipping from a Pittsburgh paper that told about Russian troops finding mass graves in Lithuania after they forced the Germans out. It was some kind of death camp. It didn't say if they were Jews, but they were certainly poor souls—1,500 men, women, and children."

"Sam, that's horrible. I never saw anything like that in our paper."

"There probably wasn't anything. Small-town papers deal with local news and big stories. Morris says even the big-city papers don't do much with that stuff. They can't verify the stories, and some people don't want to believe it. I recall reading a column some months ago that our government is very suspicious of the releases coming from the Russians. They think it's propaganda to make the Allies push harder in the west."

"So in the meantime, lots of poor, innocent people may suffer?"

"I'm afraid so."

Three

When he awoke from his nap, Jimmie smelled food coming from the kitchen. For a few seconds, he savored the smell of what he felt certain was carcass soup, and then he was tempted to investigate. Getting up from the couch, he walked into the kitchen.

"It's a whole lot warmer here, Mom," he said.

"I wouldn't wonder," Clara replied. "The oven's on, and three burners of the range, not to mention the little floor stove."

"Seems strange with all this heat, there's ice on the windows."

"You'd have to ask your father for a scientific answer, but I'd guess it has something to do with the moisture in the air from cooking and the outside temperature, which has been in the twenties all day."

"That soup really smells good. Too bad we have it only a couple times a year."

"The main thing you're smelling is turkey broth. Since we usually have turkey only for Thanksgiving and then Christmas, there's no other time of year we have the makin's."

"I guess that's the end of the turkey, then."

"Not quite. I saved enough for sandwiches for lunch for you boys and your father tomorrow. I wouldn't be surprised if Aunt Marge would like to take some back, too, so I saved a little for her."

Jimmie moved closer to the stove. "Looks like we'll have plenty of soup. Your big canner's better than three-quarters full."

"That's about right." Clara smiled.

Jimmie's such a good boy, she thought. *He always brings a smile to my face. He's ten-years old, but he'll always be my baby. I guess that's because he had such a hard time. I hated being unable to bring him home from the hospital right after he was born. Since he arrived a month early, they kept him wrapped in cotton strips for better than a week. After he started going to school, he seems to catch all the colds going 'round each winter. I keep hoping he'll catch up in size with the other kids his age, but that hasn't happened yet.*

"How about puttin' on your coat and getting a big jar of applesauce from the cellar for me?"

"OK, Mom." He walked quickly across the kitchen to retrieve his jacket from one of the hooks behind the door to the living room.

"Now take it easy. You don't have to bust anything. Remember how you tripped with the jar of peaches on the steps last summer and cut your hand?"

"I sure do. I'll be careful."

"By the way, while you're down there, would you see how many jars of green beans we have left? We go through them pretty quick."

He walked through the living room and onto the front porch before walking around the house to the cellar entrance.

I have to be careful, he thought. *That wet snow from yesterday and the overnight freeze has turned everything to ice.* He stepped carefully on the white surface, and his feet broke through with a crunch. *Not so bad.*

Boy, that sunset sure is something. Seems like the whole western sky beyond the barn is bright orange. I wonder if winter sunsets really have more color than summer, or if it just seems that way. I'm glad I don't have to be outside for long. It's cold, and Dad said it felt like snow. He's glad we brought the beef cattle in from the other side of the farm to the barn, so it'll be easier to feed them.

Jimmie opened the cellar door, went in, and turned on the light. He immediately smelled salt, sugar, and the dry rub Sam put on hams and bacon slabs to cure them.

Too bad the cooked ham slices didn't taste as good as they smelled down here, he thought. *They were so salty, they hurt my mouth.* He saw three hams still hanging from the rafters. *Getting low. Other years, we butchered the day after Thanksgiving, but Dad wanted to get the beef cattle to the barn. It sure turned cold overnight. He'll probably butcher next weekend.*

Jimmie returned to the kitchen. "Here you go, Mom. Safe and sound with the applesauce. We have twenty-three jars of green beans."

"Thank you." She smiled.

He watched her carefully place her cigarette on the edge of the table and approach the stove. She sometimes coughed a lot when she smoked.

I wonder why people call them coffin nails, he thought. *Maybe they aren't good for you. They sure do stink.*

He watched her stir the pot and the remaining turkey gravy in another pot. She opened the oven door and looked in without comment on the leftover turkey parts and stuffing being warmed.

She turned toward Jimmie. "Go to the living room and call upstairs to your Aunt Marge to say supper will be ready soon. We'll eat when your father and Reed come in from the barn."

"OK, Mom."

Finishing the task, he returned to the kitchen.

"Jimmie, can you very carefully take the plates into the dining room and set them around the table?"

"Sure, Mom. Why aren't we eating here in the kitchen?"

"When there's just the four of us, the kitchen table works fine, but with Marge here, it's a bit crowded. Anyway, she likes the fancier setting in the dining room. Maybe it reminds her of better times when she was a young woman growing up here."

Jimmie wondered about that. He was about to ask Clara to explain when the door opened, and Reed came into the kitchen carrying two large buckets of milk. He set them down and pulled off his gloves.

"Is the milking finished?" Clara asked.

"Dad's finishing up with the Jersey. He told me to bring these inside. We wouldn't have enough to fill another milk can for pickup tomorrow, and he said you wanted some cream."

"That's true. We used a lot of butter for Thanksgiving, and we're almost out. Put them in the junk room, where it's cool. Maybe after supper, Jimmie, you can crank the separator for me."

"Sure, Mom. Then we can churn butter tomorrow. Maybe there'll be enough cream left over for ice cream. We sure have plenty of ice."

"Maybe, but I wouldn't count on it. We'll have cream, but I don't know about the sugar. We'll use a lot of it for cookies and other things for Christmas. I'll have to see what's left and how many sugar ration stamps we have."

"There's always the chance Frank might have some extras at the store somebody can't use," Reed said.

It's nice of him to take my side, Jimmie thought. *He's hard to understand. He likes to tease me and call me "Squirt," but he looks after me, too. At the bus stop, when Lefty grabbed my geography book and acted like he would toss it in the creek, Reed straightened him out in a hurry.*

Reed turned sixteen the previous October. For a while, he liked to remind people that in two years or less, he'd be old enough for the service and hoped the war would last that long. Sam told him to stop saying that in front of his mother, because it upset her. Reed was tall like their father, already over six feet, with big bones, broad shoulders, but not heavy for his size. He shared Jimmie's blue eyes and blond hair.

Aunt Marge walked into the kitchen. "You'll have to excuse me for soldierin' on the job. I should've been down earlier, but I needed to correct those French tests." She smiled. "The seniors would be disappointed if they didn't get the results tomorrow." Her eyes twinkled.

"It looks like things are pretty much under control," Marge added. "Anything I can do to help?"

"I was getting ready to mash the potatoes. Can you keep an eye on the soup and the things in the oven while I do that?"

"OK. Looks like you'll have plenty of soup. Suppose there might be some left over I can take back in a jar?"

"Oh, yes. There'll be lots left over. We won't miss a quart or so. You're more than welcome to have some."

Marge, the youngest female sibling in the family, was only two years older than Sam. Her five older sisters all married, leaving her as the unclaimed treasure or the old maid in the family. In her youth, she had a serious relationship with a high-school classmate who unfortunately died in the Argonne Forest during the Great War. Subsequently, she got a college education and pursued a teaching career. She was always helpful and generous to her siblings and other family members.

Jimmie watched Aunt Marge taste the soup, nod, and stir it. He liked her, though he felt shy around her. *Maybe it's because I think of her like one of my teachers at school,* he thought. *She's always nice to me, and I can always count on nice Christmas and birthday gifts from her, but she isn't affectionate like my other aunts. I don't think she has ever given me a hug.*

She always dressed plainly, with her hair pulled back in a bun, and her clothing in dark, solid colors. Her shoes featured function over style.

She's not ugly, but she isn't pretty like Mom, he thought.

The outside door opened, and Sam came in with a bucket of milk. He hung up his winter hat and denim work coat, rubbed his thighs, and shuddered.

"It must be a good thirty degrees warmer in here. That sure feels good."

"Want me to put the milk in the junk room, Dad?" Jimmie asked.

"Sure, Son. Just be careful not to spill it. It's pretty full."

Jimmie picked up the bucket of milk and opened the door into the small room off the kitchen. It was cooler in there, and the room functioned as a pantry, so he closed the door after he went in, setting the bucket beside the separator against the far wall.

I like turning the separator to get the cream and skim milk coming out in two spouts. Maybe we'll do that after supper. This room's really full with the washing machine, rinse tubs, little drain sink, and old ice chest. It's chilly in here, too! I'd best get back in the kitchen.

Sam sat in a kitchen chair with a sigh, making eye contact with Clara, as she walked to the sink. "It looks like the meal's pretty much underway."

"That's so. By the time you're washed up, we'll be ready to put things on the table. You look tired. I hope you don't fall asleep at your plate."

"I don't figure on doing that, but I wouldn't count on much lively conversation from me after supper. Being out in the cold most of the afternoon really took it out of me."

"You shouldn't work so hard, Sam," Marge said. "There's always tomorrow."

"Yes, there is, but some things won't wait. I needed to get the rough shelters finished by the barn, since we brought in the beef cattle on Friday. One of these days, we'll get some heavy snow. What's outside right now is just a sample."

In a few minutes, all were seated at the table. Jimmie liked leftovers as much as the Thanksgiving feast itself. There was some of everything, including turkey, stuffing, gravy, mashed potatoes, and, of course, carcass soup.

Good, he thought, looking around. *There's even some of that pineapple and marshmallow stuff for dessert. I never figured out why they call it a salad.*

Sam began ladling soup.

"Why don't we say a prayer before every meal like we did at Thanksgiving?" Jimmie asked.

The adults looked at each other.

Finally, Clara replied, "Thanksgiving's a special day. It just seems right that we say a prayer to give thanks to the Lord, but there's no reason we can't do that before every meal. Some folks do. Would you like to say some words?"

"I don't think I can do that."

"I'll bet you can. It doesn't have to fancy or long like the preacher in church. Just give thanks for the food."

As Jimmie eyed his plate in silence for a few seconds, Clara looked at Reed. Her raised eyebrow told him his grin was out of place.

"Thanks for all this good food, Lord," Jimmie said. "I know this will be the best soup ever. Amen."

"That was very nice, Jimmie," Aunt Marge said. "I doubt the preacher could've done better."

As usual, the bulk of the table conversation was between the women.

"Have you decided when you'll get here for Christmas?" Clara asked Marge.

"School ends on Friday. I think that's the twenty-second. I'll have a couple things to do before I leave Munhall. It might be Saturday afternoon, depending on the train or streetcar schedule to Washington."

"That's not a problem is it, Sam?"

"Nope. I can pick you up either Saturday afternoon or evening, Marge."

"That's settled, then. Clara, have you heard from Gayle?"

"I talked to her a couple times on the phone last week and tried to convince her to spend Thanksgiving with us, but she wouldn't hear of it. She has to work at the dress shop the day before and the day after, so she felt it would be too much travel for Sam to bring her out and take her back."

"I can see her point, but what about Christmas?"

"She said she'd come, but she wasn't very enthusiastic. I'm pretty sure we'll both have to keep after her, or she'll talk herself out of it."

"I agree. She's had a tough time these last few years. Lon died in 1938 when he fell off a drilling rig, and it's not easy keeping a home together for two boys. Now both of them are in harm's way. Ralph is in a German prisoner-of-war camp, and God only knows where Rex is. He's probably somewhere in France. She won't feel any better sitting around in that little apartment alone on Christmas Day."

"It's not the same as her own boys, but from a few things she's told me, she really misses the young men in the ASTP program who lived next door to her until the program closed last spring."

"What's ASTP?" Reed asked.

"It stands for Armed Services Training Program," Sam explained. "They started it a couple years ago to provide accelerated college-level training in specific study areas with the usual military stuff for guys who have high academic scores. The idea was, it might quality them for early advancement to noncommissioned officers or even Officers Training School."

"Gayle really connected to those young fellows after they arrived in '43 for classes at the college," Clara said. "That was right after Ralph was reported missing. She made cookies for them, and they started calling her Mom. I guess they both filled empty spots for each other."

"You said they stopped the program last spring, Dad," Reed said. "Why?"

"I don't really know. It was before D-Day. Maybe they felt there would be a greater need for a sheer number of troops."

"I haven't paid much attention to the news over the weekend," Marge said. "How's the fighting going?"

"According to the radio this morning, things are a little quiet in France right now. They said the situation was a bit static. There might be a month or six-week lull, then a big push into Germany when the weather breaks."

"That sounds hopeful. Will it be over soon?"

"It's anyone's guess, but it sounds like it won't be much longer in Europe, but it's a different story in the Pacific. Those Japs are a bunch of fanatics, though MacArthur is making steady progress in the Philippines."

"I don't want to butt in," Clara said, "but it's almost six. When do you need to be in town to catch the streetcar to Pittsburgh?"

"It leaves at a quarter past seven, but I like to get there ahead of time," Marge said. "I want to be sure I get into the Pittsburgh area before it's too late. For a while, the schedule from Pittsburgh to Munhall was really messed up and unreliable after that accident two weeks ago."

"I hadn't heard about that."

"I'm surprised you didn't. It was at the junction on the Homestead-Munhall line. Several people were killed, and a whole bunch were injured. I never heard what caused it, but I have my suitcase packed, so I can be ready whenever you want to start."

"That should work. I'll just rid up a bit and do the dishes when we're back. Sam, will the roads be all right?"

"Oh, they're mostly clear. I can always put on chains if the roads are bad."

"Dad, I don't think there's much need for me to come along," Reed said. "If it's OK with everybody, I'd rather stay home. I have geometry problems I have to finish for tomorrow."

"That'll be all right," Sam said, "but you boys help your mom clear the table. I'll go start the car and let it warm up."

Everyone set to work. In a few minutes, they were in the car, backing down the lane onto the road.

"I do so enjoy coming out here," Marge said, "especially at the holidays, Sam, but I hate having you use up your gas stamps running me back and forth."

"That hasn't been a problem so far. I have a B card, since teaching is considered an essential service, and we get extra for the tractor."

Conversation was limited for the balance of the trip. There were no problems with the road or the weather, and they reached town forty-five minutes before the street car would depart. They entered the largely deserted terminal, where Marge bought a ticket.

"It's only half a block to the drugstore," Sam said with a chuckle. "I suppose everyone's too cold for a hot-fudge sundae."

"Oh, no, Dad!" Jimmie said. "It's not that cold. We left home without having dessert."

Sam looked at the women, who smiled. "There don't seem to be any strong objections, so let's go."

In a few minutes, they entered the drugstore and were greeted by the combined aroma of perfume and cologne mingled with the odor of food from the grill. They sat and soon enjoyed their ice cream.

Clara seemed reflective. "Your dad would've had a hard time with this rationing, especially the sugar."

"That's right," Marge replied. "Mom and you had to bake something every day. A meal wasn't complete for Pop if it he didn't have cake or pie for dessert."

Jimmie knew they meant his grandfather. *I haven't thought about Granddad in a long time. He died about this time of year. Yes, it was right after Thanksgiving. I remember it was the year I was in third grade.*

I can't remember him ever talking to me. He was an old, wrinkly man sitting in a rocking chair near the fireplace in the living room. When he wasn't sleeping, he was puffing on his pipe or smoking one of his long, black cigars.

"Mom, why didn't Granddad ever talk to me?" he asked.

"He did when you were just a little fellow. In his last couple of years, his health wasn't very good, and he just wanted to sit and rest. I suppose he closed his eyes and remembered your grandmother, who passed on before you were born. Maybe he was thinking about people and friends from bygone days. Granddad liked you and thought you were a good boy."

"You still are a good boy, Jimmie," Marge said. "That's important with Christmas coming."

A little while later, they saw Marge off on her return trip to Munhall, and the family drove home. Jimmie, with the back seat to himself, recalled Aunt Marge's reference to Christmas. Two years earlier, he and several classmates concluded there was no Santa Claus, though he still thought it nice to think Santa existed.

It's mean when the older kids at school tease the younger ones and say there isn't a Santa until they cry. Dad and Mom both said that Christmas for the last few years, and surely this one, aren't like they were before the war, so we shouldn't expect too much. I don't understand that. What would the war have to do with Christmas?

Before they traveled more than an hour, Jimmie fell asleep.

"I noticed when we came out of church this morning," Clara said, "you made a point of not speaking to Milo Day. He looked away as we passed. What's going on?"

"He's had a burr under his saddle for a while. I wanted to return the favor."

"That's obvious, but what's it all about?"

"It goes back to the business at the high school. He'd been on the board and was just leaving when I came on. I was the one who pushed hardest to convert that building into a consolidated primary school and bus the high-school kids into town, where they could get a decent education. It worked out well, but Milo was upset about it."

"Do you know why?"

"He'd been on the board a long time, maybe back in the twenties when they built the high school. He seemed to think of it as his building. I heard one of his nephews was a pretty good athlete on the football team and was supposed to be the big star the year we made the change, so that made me the bad guy."

"So we're talking about ego and athletics. That doesn't have much to do with education, it seems to me."

"Me, either. Sometimes, you have to move forward and ignore the bumps in the road."

"At least I know what the conflict is about."

Four

The last of the youngsters exited the bus. Because of the cold, they hurried off in different directions to get home as quickly as possible. The driver made a cautious turn to line up with the one-lane covered bridge.

Jimmie always enjoyed driving through the three covered bridges on the bus route between home and school. There was a slapping sound as the bus went over the planks. The noises were louder in the confined area.

Not everyone liked covered bridges. He remembered hearing his mom and dad talk, when she wondered if the old wooden bridges were strong enough to carry trucks and buses. Dad replied that with a war going on, he doubted there was any money to fix roads and bridges.

Once through the bridge, the driver shifted gears, and the bus climbed up the grade and away from Ten Mile Creek along the hillside bordering the tributary. At the top, he shifted, and picked up speed.

Won't be long, Jimmie thought. *I'll soon be home, or at least at the final stop.*

Glancing around, he saw only six riders on the bus, with two stops to go.

Ed Craft spoke from across the aisle. "Thanks for the turkey sandwich at lunchtime. Your mom sure knows how to fix eats."

"Oh, that's OK. She had more stuff in my lunch bucket than I could handle." *She usually fixes more than I can eat,* he realized. *Guess she's trying to fatten me up. Anyway, I feel sorry for Ed and his sisters. They have the same stuff in their lunch bucket every day—a sandwich made of two slices of homemade bread with nothing between but yellow mustard. Oh yeah. They always have an orange. Ed says they get the oranges from relief, whatever that is.*

The bus slowed to the sound of screeching brakes, as it halted at its last stop. Ed and his sisters, along with the Hickman kids, hurried off.

"See ya!" Ed called.

Harry, the driver, started the bus up the road toward the last stop and pulled a cigarette from his pocket and lit it. Jimmie watched that ritual every evening near the end of the route. As was customary, Harry reached to his left and adjusted the small, triangular window to send the smoke out of the bus. The effort was largely futile, and the smell of burning tobacco mingled with that of gasoline, orange rinds, other food, and a hint of skunk, probably from some boy's trapping efforts.

He must not be supposed to smoke while he's driving the bus, Jimmie thought. *This is the only time he does it, but it's not that important. Almost all the grown-ups I know are smokers.*

The bus negotiated the curve by the Eppley farmhouse and entered the long straightaway that ended at another curve near Jimmie's house. He had a good view of their property for the last quarter-mile. The house, barn, and outbuildings were arranged almost in a row perpendicular to the road at the foot of a hill, topped by a fruit orchard and crop and hayfields beyond. With the leaves off the trees, it was possible to see the remains of the large wagon at the edge of the orchard. According to Sam, it was the last of the huckster wagons Granddad used when he was in that business before he got into oil and natural gas drilling.

Neither the barn nor most of the outbuildings had ever been painted, so they had the common gray shade of weathered lumber. Only the house and wagon shed, used as a garage, were painted white.

Jimmie recalled Sam saying he guessed the original portion of the house was over 100 years old. It was added to several times until it became one of the larger homes in the area. Several tall pine trees towered over it, and Jimmie thought it looked really nice. He knew, though, that his mother worried about damage to the house if one of the trees fell during a windstorm.

Shortly thereafter, the bus slowed for its final stop. Jimmie grabbed his books and lunch bucket and walked down the aisle. His timing was perfect, and he reached the steps just as the bus stopped. The door sprang open, and he went down the two steps and out.

"See you tomorrow, Jimmie," Harry said.

"Yep." As he stepped off the bus, Jimmie was greeted by a familiar, dependable sight. Nicky, the white-and-black family dog, which Sam always described as a product of questionable parentage, was waiting a few feet off the road. Wiggling and jumping, he welcomed Jimmie home. Carol often commented on the uncanny way Nicky always knew when the bus would arrive and always asked to be let out several minutes in advance.

Jimmie greeted the dog with a few words and a pat on the head. Nicky turned and led the way up the lane toward the house.

Once inside, he tossed his books on the sofa and went into the kitchen to hang his coat on a hook on the wall behind the open living room door.

"Hi, Mom." He sat down to remove his overshoes.

Clara sat at the kitchen table, lighting a cigarette, a cup of coffee in front of her. "Hi, Jimmie. How'd school go today?"

"OK, I guess."

She smiled, knowing only specific interrogation would produce any explicit information. "This was the day to buy savings stamps, wasn't it?"

"Yep."

"How many did you get today?"

"I had thirty cents, so that got me three stamps."

"Are you close to filling up your book?"

"I have a page and a half to go. It'll probably take another month to fill the book and get my war bond."

"That's good. We can put it in the lockbox at the bank with the others. When it matures, it'll be worth twenty-five dollars." She paused. "You never told me if you like the building where you're going to school now. I guess it's really different."

She remembered the controversy over closing the five one-room schoolhouses in favor of using the newer high-school building as a consolidated elementary school, then busing the high school students to town.

"It was hard getting used to at first. There were so many more kids, and changing classes was new. The area out back for recess is a lot smaller than we had at the old school up the road. There isn't much grass. It's mostly dirt and gravel. If you run and fall, you'll get skinned pretty good. With cold weather coming, the building will be a lot better."

"How's that?"

"There's a big, old furnace in the basement, with heat registers in all the rooms. The old place got really cold with just a pot-bellied stove in the middle of the room. If your desk was near the outside wall, one leg would be warm, and the other would be cold. I won't miss that."

She smiled and nodded. "Did you start any new projects at school today?"

"Yes. Miss Thompson got everyone started on Christmas coloring projects.

"That sounds nice. What kind of pictures? Did everyone have the same thing?"

"No. She had four or five we could choose from. There were several copies of each she made from the hectograph. There was a Santa Claus with a big pack of presents, a Christmas tree with bulbs and packages under it, a manger scene with baby Jesus, and a couple others."

"Which one did you choose?"

"The Christmas tree."

"That'll be nice. What will she do with them?"

"She said she'll pick the best ones and put them in windows, kinda like decorations. 'Course, that'll be the girls. They always get picked for the best coloring."

"Maybe not. I've seen some of your work that's pretty good. Maybe you're just in too much of a hurry to finish, so you mess up near the end. I'll bet if you went a little slower, you'd have a winner."

The suggestion produced no response from him, just a brief pause in the conversation. Clara inhaled from her cigarette before continuing.

"Anything else? I guess there'll be a Christmas program. Have they set a time for that?"

"Miss Thompson hasn't said, but everyone says it's always on the last day before Christmas vacation."

"Will you have a part in it?"

"I don't know. I hope not, but everybody usually has something to do. She said something about having a group of three boys and three girls sing *Jingle Bells*. I sure hope I don't get stuck with that."

Clara saw Jimmie felt uncomfortable talking about the Christmas program, so she changed the subject after taking a final drag on her cigarette and stubbing it out in the ashtray.

"I almost forgot," Clara said. "Before you take off your arctics, I have a little chore for you. There's about an hour of daylight left. Your dad would like you to get those three small cedar trees in the orchard beyond where the transparent apples are. He cut them down, and they aren't very big. He thought you could tie them to your sled and bring them down out back of the kitchen."

"Sure, I can, but what's he want them for?"

"He wants to start making wreaths. He always makes some for here and up at the cemetery for your grandparents' graves. Your aunts and Uncle Lou might want some, and who knows who else? He likes working with cedar best. They take longer to make than the long-needle pine, but they're nice and full."

"OK. I'd better get going." He pulled on his coat, hat, and gloves and walked back outside.

At the wagon shed, he got his sled and some binder twine to tie the cedar trees. The trip up to the orchard wasn't far, but it took time to deal with the slippery snow, because he kept breaking through the crust.

The cedar trees were only a few inches longer than his sled, making it easy to tie them on securely. The trip downhill was much easier than the one up. In a few minutes, he was finished.

I might as well do my other chores before I go back in. I can take the slop bucket to the hog pen and feed the chickens. Reed and Dad will be home soon, and they'll bring in the milk cows. I'll have time to listen to Terry and the Pirates *before supper.*

Sam pushed back from the table with a satisfied look. "That was a good supper. That beef stew and those drop dumplings really stick to your ribs. I hope they won't put me to sleep too soon. I'd like to catch the news."

"I hope this doesn't raise a sour note," Clara said, "but I'm expecting a couple women to come over this evening to work on the quilt. I had the parlor door open all afternoon to warm it up a little. Did you get the rest of the lines laid out for stitching?"

"Yes. The balance are penciled in. You've got only a foot and a half to go before you finish. Maybe you'll see the end tonight."

"That depends on who shows up. We need to finish it soon. Christmas will be on us before you know it, and we need to get the frames out of the parlor for the tree."

"Who are you expecting?"

"Just Ester and Francis. Three's about all you can get comfortably along the side. Anyway, I have to keep moving. They might arrive any minute. Will everyone help clear the table?"

The family did it quickly.

"I think I heard a car come up the lane," Clara said. "That's Frank dropping off Ester and Francis. Reed, can you and Jimmie do the dishes for me, so I can get going on the quilt?"

"Sure, Mom," Reed said. "I'll wash, and he can dry."

A moment later, they heard the front door open, and a piercing voice call, "Anybody home?"

"Yes, we are, Francis," Clara said. "You ladies are right on time. Why don't you go in the parlor, and I'll catch up in a minute. Just put your coats on the sofa."

A few minutes later, all three women sat at the quilting frame and began their evening's work.

"Ester, did Frank mention anything to you about what he heard at the store about Max Lindley?" Francis asked.

"No, but he doesn't usually bring home much information he's heard unless it deals with someone around here. Max Lindley? Is he one of the Lindleys up around Prosperity?"

"Yes. He's Herb and Barbara's oldest. I heard something on the phone this morning."

Clara and Ester exchanged a smile. It was common knowledge that Francis spent a lot of her time on the party line, listening to other people's conversations. She didn't disguise the fact or feel any shame at invading people's privacy.

"What did you learn?" Clara asked.

"It was difficult to hear. There must've been other people rubberin' on the line. You must know he graduated from college and was working for one of the Pittsburgh department stores when he was drafted early on. He was sent to an Army camp in Georgia in '42 for infantry training. I don't recollect the name. Seems to me it started with a B.

"Anyway, early on, he got in some stuff that wasn't about fighting. It was some kind of publicity. He ran a radio station and a newspaper at the camp. I never knew they did that kinda stuff. The way I heard it, when the big shots came down from Washington, it was his job to see all their arrangements were made. Anyway, he never got assigned to a combat unit the whole time."

She paused, then continued. "I believe it was her mother talking to his aunt that I heard. They were concerned that with all the casualties since D-Day, and all the replacements that were needed, his number would be up. What his mother was saying was that he dodged the bullet again and would stay there for the time being."

"I guess he was doing a necessary job," Ester said. "If he was doing something that kept him from being killed, all the better. What do you think, Clara?"

"I agree with you. It's just a drop in the bucket, but we've had a lot of young men from around here wounded or killed. Enough is enough."

The three women concentrated on their work.

"Here's some news, though it's not unexpected," Ester said. "Frank got notified today that the new food ration stamps will come in the week after Christmas."

"Then I guess we'll start using them at the first of the year," Clara said.

"Yes. That's right."

The conversation stopped for a minute.

"I seldom hear you talk about your family, Clara," Ester said. "Do you expect to see any of them around Christmas?"

"That's hard to say. I know for sure I won't see either of my brothers. Henry lives in Chicago and works for one of the railroads. His wife's family is from out that way, so I don't expect him to come here. He's twelve years older than I. I'm lucky to hear from him once a year.

"Paul, my other brother, has some kind of government job with the Agriculture Department out in Oklahoma. I'm sure he won't be back. The only possibility is Grace, my baby sister. They live down by Point Marion, but they don't own a car, so if we have enough stamps for gas, maybe we'll visit them. I'd love to see her two little girls."

"We've been making good time this evening," Francis said. "I'm almost at the end of my section."

"Yes," Clara agreed. "Progress has been really good. I see it's almost nine, so I suppose Frank will toot his horn soon. If we don't finish tonight, I'm sure I can find time over the next couple days to complete things. Let's quit and go to the kitchen for a piece of cake before you leave."

After Ester and Francis left, Clara sat in the kitchen, smoking a cigarette. *I'm glad the quilt is almost finished,* she thought. *By the end of the week, I can have it done, and we'll be able to take down the frames and put them away. Then there's nothing standing in the way of Christmas.*

Five

The following day after evening chores, the family sat at the kitchen table for the evening meal.

"I hope you enjoy the ham," Clara said. "There may be a little left for breakfast meat, but that's about it."

"If all goes well, I plan to butcher this Saturday," Sam said. "Maybe by this time next week, we'll have fresh pork of some kind."

"That'll be nice. How many will you butcher?" Clara asked.

"I'm planning to do three. I wouldn't want to tackle any more. I've already asked Allison and Dan to help, but there's a lot of work after they help me do the heavy work of getting it down to quarters. I have to cut all the roasts, chops, ribs, and sausage parts."

"That's so, but it sure is a godsend. The price of meat's so high, I can't imagine how ordinary folks afford it.

"Sam, I didn't mention this to you when you came home from school, but Grace called this afternoon."

"That's nice. You haven't spoken with her for a while. How's your little sister doing?"

"Their situation is improving. Since Larry landed that trucking job with the coal company last spring, their finances have improved a lot. That's the first steady job he's had in their six years of marriage."

"1938 wasn't the best time to get married from an economic standpoint, but that's not much consideration if you have two people who can't live apart. Good thing he's working for the coal company. That's probably considered a critical job."

"What do you mean?"

"I read in the paper a couple days ago that on February first, they're start drafting men in the twenty-six-to-thirty-eight age group. I guess they figure they're gonna need a lot of cannon fodder when they close in on the Japs. Men in critical jobs might be exempt."

"Thank God for that. It sure would be nice to see them and those two little girls," she said wistfully. "It's been several months since we visited them, and they don't own a car to come see us."

"We'll have to see. It's a long drive down to Point Marion, but maybe I'll have enough ration stamps for gas to make the trip near the end of the month."

He pushed his chair back from the table. "It's almost six. I'll pass on dessert. I want to see if I can catch the news."

A few minutes later, he sat beside the radio after dialing it to KDKA. He endured commercials and local news, then the broadcast turned to events concerning the war.

Reports from the Associated Press and individual correspondents having to do with the military situation on the western front in Europe are generally positive. U.S. ground forces continue to hammer the Siegfried Line and have advanced within only a few miles of the Ruhr River, which, along with the Rhine River, constitute the enemy's best natural barriers defending their homeland.

At the same time, Patton's Third Army in the south made significant advances threatening the Saar Basin, which is second only to the Ruhr as a source of Germany's war might.

Elsewhere, massive Allied air raids on German oil refineries resulted in heavy damage, although several heavy bombers were lost in the effort. In the east, Russian forces continued their advances in the Trans-Danube Front.

In the Philippines, Japanese efforts to reinforce their garrisons on Leyte were thwarted with the loss of several ships and an estimated 25,000 troops. In Canada, the demonstrations of the French-Canadian troops against being deployed overseas seem to have abated.

All in all, Sam thought, *things are going well. It'll take awhile for them to finish supper and clean up. I can't get going on the wreaths until they're done. Might as well take a little nap.*

Closing his eyes, he settled back in the chair.

My legs are so tired, it seems like I've been walking forever. I'm thankful there's only two or three inches of snow on the ground. Any more, and the walking would be really tough. It's bad enough there are all these evergreen trees along with saplings and brush. I have to zigzag in the general direction of where the platoon should be.

Uh-oh. Sounds like another incoming gift from the Krauts. I'd better hit the deck. Son of a bitch! What a hit! That wasn't a mortar. Must've been an eighty-eight. I'd better keep going.

Here's a dirt road. It's not much better than a trail, but it's something to follow. I smell smoke. Something's burning up ahead. It sure would be nice to get warm for the first time in days.

Good Lord. It's a Jeep, or what's left of one. For Christ's sake, there are two bodies in it, but they're more like two lumps of charcoal. I guess that means a couple more telegrams and a couple more gold stars in somebody's window.

What a mess. The windshield's been blown off to one side. What the hell? A gas-rationing sticker? That doesn't make sense.

Gotta keep moving. Wait! That's small-arms fire. Maybe it's some of our guys. There's a little clearing to the right.

Oh, my God! There are eight bodies in a row. Shit! They aren't Germans. Those are GIs. I hear someone coming. It's four Krauts! I'm in big trouble.

"Kapitan, sieht es aus wie wir verpasst. Was jetzt?"

"Wir konnen nicht mit Gefangenen belastigt werden. Shoot ihn."

Oh, my God. They're going to shoot me!

"No! Stop!"

Sam woke with a start, shaking and sweating.

What a hell of a dream. No, that was a nightmare. It was really screwy. I was never in the military. A gas-ration sticker on a Jeep in the middle of nowhere? Stupid.

What a weird dream. Usually, I can relate my dreams to something that happened to me or that I heard about. Why would I dream of being in the military? Things are going pretty good in Europe. Maybe it'll wind down by the end of the year. A gas-ration sticker on a Jeep? How dumb is that?

No use wasting time over a dream. I'd better get back into the kitchen and start making wreaths.

Later, family members were dispersed throughout the house in different activities. Jimmie and Reed sat at the dining room table to do their homework. Clara was in the downstairs bedroom, darning and patching worn clothing. Sam was in the kitchen, making Christmas wreaths.

"That finishes my arithmetic," Jimmie announced.

"So that's all you've got for tonight, Squirt?" Reed asked.

"Yep."

"You're lucky. I finished my biology, but I still have geometry to do, and it gives me fits."

Jimmie left the table and walked into the kitchen, where he was greeted by the smell of cedar and foliage. Sam sat at the table, almost hidden by a huge pile of cedar twigs.

Jimmie liked to watch his father make wreaths. The round wooden frames were made earlier in the year from saplings. Sam heated them in hot water and carefully bent them around a large bucket before wiring them into a perfect circle. As Jimmie watched, Sam selected an appropriate-sized twig and wired it into place. There was plenty of overlap, which gave a full appearance.

"Golly, Dad. It looks like you've got enough cedar to make a dozen wreaths."

"It may look that way, Jimmie, but there's only enough for one or two. You have to use a lot to make them look really full and nice."

"Why do you do this every year? It's a lot of work."

"Maybe it is, but I enjoy it. The folks I make them for seem to appreciate it, and I like making things look nice for the holidays. It's my way to show a little respect for my mother and father by putting a decoration on their gravesite." He looked up and grinned. "Is that reasons enough?"

"I guess so."

Sam looked away and shook his head thoughtfully. "I don't know anyone else who makes wreaths this way anymore. I'm the only one left." He paused. "When I'm dead and gone, there won't be anyone around to make a wreath to put on my grave."

Jimmie didn't know what to say, so he walked to the side of the kitchen and sat in a chair. *That sounds so sad. It's funny he'd say that now. Christmas is supposed to be a happy time.*

Clara walked in. "I heard you had the news on, Sam. How are things going?"

"Pretty well. There's a fair amount of activity with the Germans. There's a couple places where our boys have pushed near the border. Lowell Thomas offered the opinion that the Allies were taking it easy and waiting for supplies and reinforcements to catch up with the front."

"How about in the Pacific?"

"They didn't say much about that other than we're still making progress in the Philippines. Oh, yes. There was a big air raid on Tokyo. A whole bunch of B-29s went there. They said there was heavy damage to the Jap airplane plants."

"I haven't heard from my cousin, Carolyn, in a while. Her middle son, Paul, is out there somewhere, but at least he's in the navy, not crawling around the jungle somewhere getting shot at."

There was a pause in the conversation.

"Sam, did you tell Jimmie he might have pine orders?" she asked.

"I forgot. Son, three or four of the women teachers asked me if they could get some pine from us for decorating like last year. It'd be a chance for you to make a bit of money to buy Christmas presents. What do you think?'

Jimmie hopped to his feet with a big smile. "That's great news! I'd have time to take my sled up the hollow and bring back at least one bundle after I get home from school. There's Saturday, too. How much could I make?"

"Hard to say for sure. The first ones who asked would be a start, and I figure word will get around. You'll soon have more customers. I won't charge too much to taking it to school in the car," he added with a grin.

Jimmie smiled at his dad's teasing. *Maybe I'll get enough to buy Mom a Christmas present. She's been wanting a round mirror for the center of the dining room table. It probably costs a lot, though.*

"That's great," Jimmie said. "I'll start tomorrow evening as soon as I get home from school."

"Good. I'll tell them the pine is on its way. Remember, you've still got regular chores every evening."

"That's settled," Clara said. "You've made a good start so far this evening. How many wreaths did you plan to make?"

"I thought I'd make three, one for the front door, one for the door from the outside into the parlor, and one for Mom and Dad's grave. If I run out of time, I might cut out the one for the parlor. Nobody ever comes in that way. We might go down county in the next couple weeks, and it'd be nice to have one for your folks' grave. What do you think?"

"That sounds like a plan. It's true no one comes in through the parlor, but a wreath on the door would look nice to people driving by. Will you do something for the fireplace mantel like last year?"

"Yeah. I was thinking about something made of wood I could drill holes in for candles and place pine around it. Do we have any red candles?"

"I think so. I'll have to look. I'll check for wide ribbon to make bows for the wreaths, too."

Jimmie listened to the conversation with interest. "Are we going to have outside colored lights this year, Dad?"

"The answer to that is maybe. I have only that short string of blue lights. The bulbs were OK when I put them away last year, but I'll have to repair the wires. They looked pretty shabby. If I can cobble 'em together, we'll try to rig 'em on the small white pine along the road."

"Maybe we could get new lights?"

"Prospects for that aren't good, Son. Money's tight, and other things we need are more important. I haven't seen much in the stores in the way of lights or Christmas decorations. With everything going into the war effort, luxuries are limited. I sure don't have the money or connections to buy things on the black market."

"Black market? What's that?"

"It's hard to explain." He paused. "It's a way for rich people to get things that are hard to come by because of the war. They pay two or three times what they would usually cost. The government made it against the law to buy or sell certain items, because the materials or the workers are needed to make things our soldiers need."

"That doesn't sound very nice."

"You're right. It isn't. I guess that's why it's called black."

"Speaking of things that are hard to come by," Clara said, "the supply of cigarettes is low. Will you have time this evening to roll some?"

"I was thinking about that. I've had about enough of the wreath-making business this evening. As soon as I clean up this mess, I'll get out the rolling machine and the Bugler tobacco and get to work. I'll have enough for both of us in short order."

Clara, walking into the living room, found the boys sitting down. Reed read the current issue of *Boy's Life*. Jimmie worked on his scrapbook that was filled with pictures of war machines—aircraft, tanks, and ships—cut from magazines.

"That's starting to look nice, Jimmie," she said. "It's getting pretty full. We need to get more pages." She paused. "It's getting late. You two need to get on up to bed. It'll be time to roll out before you know it."

"OK, Mom," Reed said. "Come on, Squirt. You're first in the bathroom."

After Reed and Jimmie went upstairs, Clara picked up papers and magazines, returned other items to their proper places, and began the evening ritual of winding the mantel clock. When she returned to the kitchen, she sat at the table opposite Sam, reached across, and retrieved a freshly rolled cigarette.

"By the look of it," Sam said, "it seems you have something on your mind."

Clara lit the cigarette, inhaled, and exhaled smoke, coughing twice to clear her throat. "As a matter of fact, I do. Christmas will be here before you know it. We need to think about what we'll get the boys. I suppose we'll visit Lou and Bonnie on Christmas night like other years, but we shouldn't go empty handed. I've been looking through the Sears catalog for ideas."

Sam scratched his head. "That's quite a mouthful. The main thing is the boys. You can get the rest yourself. You usually do. Did you have anything in mind for the boys?"

"There are a couple of items of clothing. Reed could use a new long-sleeved sweater. His old one has several snags. Jimmie's at the age where he's moving from knickers to long pants. I'd like to get him one good pair of long pants for Sunday and dressing up. He'll have to make do with knickers for the rest of the school year, then we can do away with those next year."

"Sounds good. Jimmie will be on cloud nine with long pants. Anything else?"

"They both need a couple new shirts and socks. Beyond clothes, I'm stuck."

"I have an idea. The other day, when I stopped at the tire place to pick up those recaps, I looked in the windows of Scott's Sporting Goods and saw some nice-looking ice skates."

"You think they'd be interested?"

"Yes. I've heard them both talking about the kids at Plum Sock skating on the creek."

"Are they expensive?"

"Not cheap. The hockey skates run between four and six dollars, depending on size. Figure skates are twice that."

"At that price, Christmas will be costly."

"They'll only be young once. We ought to stretch things a bit."

Clara took a deep drag from her cigarette. "Maybe if you'd gotten a decent price for those two young steers you sold to Ezra Lindley last month, we wouldn't have to stretch our money so hard."

"Well, I'll be damned. You've still got that stuck in your craw? You don't seem to understand that the price of beef was down. You never get as much in fall as you do in summer."

"All I know, Sam, is that you must be the easiest mark in the county. Everyone seems to be able to beat you down on the price of everything from livestock to grain."

"Damn it all! It would be nice if you gave someone credit for trying. Instead, all you do is criticize." He almost said more but shook his head.

"Clara, I've had a long day, and I sure as shit have had enough of your bellyaching. Maybe when you don't have a burr under your saddle, we can have an intelligent discussion about this."

Standing, he left the kitchen.

Six

"I think the weather's going to be with us for today," Sam said.

"Yes," Clara replied. "It's cold and crisp, but at least it's not frigid. We aren't supposed to get snow, are we?"

"I don't think so. It's cloudy, but it doesn't feel like snow."

"I hope the weather holds for a few more days. I've been wanting to get to Pittsburgh for shopping before Christmas, and next weekend could be the last chance. It'll be good to get fresh meat. The last time I was in at the frozen-food locker plant, I saw only a few pieces of beef left. With sirloin steak at twenty-nine cents a pound at Margo's Meat Market, we won't be buying any. We can get along on the pork and chicken until you butcher that beef in March."

"I'll go see how the fire's doing and if the water's starting to boil or is at least good and hot. You can get the boys up in a little bit. It's getting light, and I have to go after Allison and Dan soon."

"Do you know what they want for helping out?"

"Pretty much the usual. Dan doesn't keep hogs, and Allison doesn't have any ready for butchering this year. Both said they'd be happy with a ham and side meat for bacon. They both like smoked meat, and Allison will cure them in his smokehouse. It's all set."

"It's a blessing they can help you."

"Yes. It certainly is. They've both been butchering a lot longer than I have."

"Are they about the same age?"

"No. Dan's getting pretty long in the tooth. He must be in his sixties, but Allison's only about ten years older than I am. He was in the last war. He and his brother, Lon, Gayle's husband, enlisted together, and they spent their time in the Pacific Northwest, cutting lumber. The Army needed it to build barracks or something."

Sam left the kitchen, and Clara considered the day. *It'll be a busy day, and a long one.* She smiled, knowing the boys would be easy to wake that morning. Butchering was one of the events in the life of a farm family that broke the tedium of the normal routine. There was a certain excitement about things that happened only once a year, like thrashing and butchering. Those events also brought in other people to help with the work, which added to the exhilaration and uniqueness of the day.

She poured another cup of coffee and lit a cigarette. *I'd better quit daydreaming and get those boys up. As soon as I get them fed and out, I'll have to start making things for dinner.*

She was right. Soon after she called up the back stairs, Reed and Jimmie came down and sat at the kitchen table, helping themselves to buckwheat cakes and meat.

"I sure do like this maple syrup, Mom," Reed said. "I hope we don't run out before spring."

"I think we'll make it. There are a couple more jugs down in the cellar."

Clara recalled that when the family returned to the farm, Sam told her it was many years since the sugar maples had been tapped to make syrup. The hard times of the Depression were followed by food rationing because of the war, which changed all that. Anything that could be produced on a farm for consumption, barter, or sale wasn't overlooked.

The boys quickly finished breakfast and started pulling on outer clothing.

"Remember your bib overalls and galoshes," Clara said. "It'll be wet and muddy out there."

"OK, Mom," they replied in unison.

"You're right on time. I hear a car coming up the lane. That must be your father returning with Allison and Dan."

The boys bolted out the kitchen door and soon stood near the butchering fire with Sam and the other two men. The wind shifted, and smoke from the fire blew into Jimmie's eyes, making him step aside. The water in the two big cast-iron kettles was steaming, and Jimmie wondered if it was hot enough. Sam would know.

Sam walked over and dipped water from a kettle with a small pan, holding it near his face, and nodded.

"That's ready. As soon as we get enough in the barrel for scalding, Reed and Jimmie, I want you to go to the pump by the cow stable and bring in four or five buckets for the kettles. We'll need a lot more hot water before we're done."

Water was transferred from the kettles to the barrel, which leaned at an angle to the side on the far side of the wooden platform, where the butchering would begin.

The three men and two boys walked briskly to the hog pen. Sam carried a twenty-two rifle.

"Reed, do you want to do the honors?" Sam asked.

"Sure, Dad."

"All right. Let's start with the big sow with the round white area on her side. Just like I told you. Wait till she looks at you, then right between the eyes and up a little."

"OK."

A few seconds later, Reed fired, and the animal immediately fell. Allison and Sam quickly stepped over the board fence into the pen. With a long knife, Allison expertly slit the animal's throat. Blood gushed from a severed artery. Sam was ready with a pail to catch the blood.

When the flow seemed to falter, he thrust the boning knife into the pig's mouth and twisted. Once secured, it served as a handle by which the beast could be pulled from the pen to a small sled hitched behind the tractor. In minutes, the burden was transported to the wooden platform by the kettles.

"Jimmie, I have a job for you," Sam said. "Take this pail with blood into the house and have your mother put it in the junk room. Be careful not to spill it."

"Ugh. What will we do with the blood?"

"We won't do anything with it. One of the male teachers at school whose family comes from the old country uses it to make blood pudding, sort of like sausage. Take this. We have to move fast."

With considerable effort, the men manhandled the animal into the barrel of hot water head first, then pulled it out and placed the back end in. Once the hog was pulled onto the wooden platform, the men set to work with bell hog scrapers to remove the hair.

Jimmie returned from the house. He and his brother stood nearby, watching intently. Without pausing his work, Sam spoke.

"See how we're doing this?" he asked. "It doesn't require much pressure, and it's important to hold the scraper at the right angle. You want to cut off the hair without cutting the hide."

It took time. At intervals, more hot water was poured on areas where the hair was especially resistant to removal.

When the men were satisfied with that stage of the work, it was time to hang the pig from the steel pipe apparatus to one side.

"Jimmie, bring one of those gambrels on the end of the workbench in the wagon shed."

He ran off. *It's a funny name for an old piece of really hard wood a few feet long that's been whittled down at the ends*, he thought. *Guess it has to be called something.*

Returning, he watched his father carefully cut a slit between the tendon and leg bone just above both rear hooves. The gambrel was inserted into the legs, and the animal was suspended in the air a foot off the ground, as the men thoroughly cleaned it on the outside.

The head was removed, and the abdominal cavity was opened, with only the heart and liver saved.

"Reed, get the metal bushel tub in the wagon shed to catch the guts."

"OK, Dad."

Finally, Sam took a meat saw and cut the length of the backbone. The two halves were ready for further reduction of the meat portions of various types.

"That went pretty smoothly," Sam said. "Let's hang these halves in the shed and get back out for the next one."

They repeated the process two more times. By midday, three hogs were butchered.

"Jimmie," we're just about finished here," Sam said. "How about you going to the house to tell your mom we'll be in to eat in a few minutes? Maybe you can help her with something."

When Jimmie entered the kitchen, warm, steamy air greeted him. He glanced toward the stove and saw all four burners had pots of food on them. Serving dishes sat on the kitchen table, waiting to be filled.

"Dad said to tell you they'd be ready to eat in a few minutes. Anything I can do to help?"

"Yes. I can use your help. Take off your overalls, coat, and galoshes."

Jimmie and Clara busily filled serving dishes with mashed potatoes and other vegetables and carried them into the dining room. Fried chicken was removed from the skillets and put on the meat platter. The remaining food items included bread, margarine, gravy, pickles, and relishes.

Almost as if on cue, Sam, Dan, Allison, and Reed entered the kitchen from outside.

"Looks like you're all ready for us, Clara," Sam said.

"Yes. Just about everything is on the table. By the time you fellows are washed up, we'll be all set."

There was very little conversation during the meal. The men and boys were thankful to be inside, out of the cold. They'd been working at hard, physical labor for several hours and needed a break and food.

When dessert was served, Clara asked, "Did you get as much done this morning as you hoped?"

"Yes," Sam said. "We did well. We got the three done I hoped for. Allison and Dan will be ready to go after the meal. Could you take them in the car? I have a lot of cutting to do, then there's wrapping and getting ready to grind sausage this afternoon or evening. I'll be busy all weekend."

"I can do that," she replied. "I don't mind driving, as long as I don't have to contend with ice on the road."

"Good. That's settled. You fellows OK with those hams and side meat?"

"Those are fine," Allison said.

Dan nodded.

"It'll be good to have fresh meat," Allison added. "We've been out for some time. Those ration stamps don't go very far."

"Not only that," Sam said, "but there seem to be meat shortages in some areas. I read in the paper the other day that OPA charged some meat suppliers in the Philadelphia area with selling their products above the ceiling prices."

"What's OPA, Dad?" Reed asked.

"It's a government outfit called the Office of Price Administration. They try to keep wages and prices from going too far. It's part of the war effort. I hope they fold up after the war. It doesn't seem right for the government to stick its nose into such things."

"Anyway," Allison said, "you can't beat the taste of home-cured meat. You sure you don't want me to take a couple of your hams with me? There's plenty of room in my smokehouse."

"Thanks just the same. We're used to the taste of the sugar cure. I may use salt on one of them."

As the men stood, Clara asked Dan, "Is your niece, Opal, still working at Mercy Hospital in Pittsburgh? How does she like it?"

Dan smiled. "She liked it well enough, but she left last April. The government had a big recruiting drive for nurses. They probably knew the invasion was comin', and they would need 'em. The pay was pretty good, so she figured she might have a chance to see new places. She's an Army nurse now somewhere in England. Her mom says she likes it."

"I hope she's safe. Our young people are seeing places and doing things because of the war that folks a generation ago couldn't have dreamed about."

Later, as Clara drove from the lane to take Allison and Dan to their homes, Sam and the boys returned to the butchering area.

"Dad, look!" Jimmie said. "Nicky got into the gut bucket!"

The family dog had a piece of intestine in its mouth, trying to pull it from the bucket.

"Nothing to worry about, Jimmie," Sam said, laughing. "He'll either give up or decide it isn't tasty. He can't seem to remember from year to year."

Sam gave his assistants work assignments. "Reed, I'd like you to help me get the rest of this one we cut for Dan and Allison over to the makeshift table. You can start cleaning around the fire, dump any water left in the big kettles, and push over the scalding barrels. Careful you don't burn yourself.

"Jimmie, take it easy for a few minutes. It won't take me long to work some of this hide loose, then you can start cutting it into strips and skinning off the fat. Get one of the butcher knives. You seen it done before and have helped. Just be careful and don't cut yourself."

Jimmie soon accumulated a large pile of fat chunks. "Dad, I don't have any more room left at this end of the table. If I cut more, they'll fall off into the mud."

"I can see that. You'll have to go back to the house and get a milk bucket to bring in the fat. Better get two. Your mother will be back soon, and she'll want to get that on the stove in the big container and render it down to lard."

"OK, Dad."

The work continued throughout the afternoon. The two boys needed little direction, because they'd done it in previous years. By the time the sun set, much had been done. The hams, shoulders, and side meat were in the cellar, ready to be cured. The loins, chops, and loose meat destined for sausage were in another secure outbuilding to be dealt with over the next few days.

Supper was quiet, almost somber. The hours of hard physical labor during butchering, followed by the never-to-be-neglected milking and feeding of livestock, were tiring. Coming in from temperatures below freezing to the kitchen's humid warmth was welcome and made even more agreeable by the odor of melting hog fat.

"It's been a long, tiring day for all of us," Sam said. "In the long run, it's worth it."

"No doubt about it," Clara said, exhaling smoke from her cigarette. "You should take the day off tomorrow to rest. As cold as it is, there's no rush to finish."

"I was considering that. Maybe we could ride down to Waynesburg after dinner."

Seven

As the family finished their noonday meal, Clara asked, "Did you boys get along OK at Sunday school this morning?"

"Yep," Reed said. "Everything was pretty much as usual."

"How about you, Jimmie? Did you remember your Bible verse?"

"Sure did, Mom. 'A soft answer turneth away wrath.' Most of the kids were surprised, since they didn't know my real name is James. Only three letters to go."

The others smiled.

"I'm glad you did well. You boys always make me proud. Your dad and I are going to Waynesburg this afternoon for a while. Jimmie, I think you should come with us. How about you, Reed?"

"I'd just as leave stay here. Maybe I'll walk back to the church and play Ping-Pong. What's happening in Waynesburg?"

"I thought it would be nice to visit your Uncle Paul and Aunt Ethel. It's been some time since we were together. We might visit the cemetery, too."

Later, Jimmie and his parents walked out to the car to start their afternoon trip. A few clouds floated in the blue sky, and the air was cold and crisp.

As Sam backed the car down the lane, he remarked, "We need a change of scenery, so I'm going by way of Ruff Creek and Route 19."

For the first several miles, there was little conversation. They didn't take that route often, so Jimmie found many new things to look at. He recognized Allison's farm, but no one was outside. Soon, they came into the small village of Ruff Creek. Sam pulled up to a stop sign where they would turn onto the main route to Waynesburg.

"Look, Dad!" Jimmie said. "There's a soldier. Maybe he needs ride."

"Could be. From where he's standing, he might be going in our direction. Roll down your window, Clara."

"Hello there, Young Fellow," Sam called. "Do you need a lift?"

The serviceman walked quickly to the car. "Why, yes, I do. I'm tryin' to get to Waynesburg."

"That's where we're going. Hop in."

Once the man was in the car, he said, "I'm Roy Sibert. I have a few days' leave, and I'm tryin' to get home to visit the folks before I have to go back overseas. It's nice and warm in here. I stood out there awhile, and it's cold."

"I'm surprised," Sam said. "I thought folks were pretty good about picking up you military fellows."

"They usually are, but where I was dropped off last was a pretty bad spot. There's a curve, and the cars move pretty fast down the road. They were past me before they saw me."

"Been in long?"

"Yeah. I enlisted the week after Pearl Harbor. I ended up in the Army Air Force as a bombardier. I got my twenty-five missions in last summer. After a while, they sent me back, and I went to school, working with aerial photographs and how to choose targets. I'll go back over, but no more combat missions, thank the Lord."

"I'd say you've done more than your share."

They soon reached the outskirts of town and descended a long hill past a well-groomed park.

"Well, Clara, there's your alma mater over on the left," Sam said.

"What's an alma mater?" Jimmie asked.

"That's how you refer to a college or university that you graduated from," Clara said. "That's where I went to school."

"You folks can drop me off anywhere on Main Street," Roy said. "I can make it from there."

"Where do you live?"

"It's out in Bucktown."

"That's another mile and a half. We aren't in a rush. We'll drop you off."

Following the airman's directions, they soon pulled up in front of a modest two-story house, where Roy got out and stood near the open door.

"It's really swell of you folks to give me a ride. I really appreciate it. Wait a minute." He reached into his coat pocket and handed something to Jimmie. "Here's a souvenir for you. I have some extras."

Jimmie stared with wide eyes at an Eighth Air Force shoulder patch. "Thanks a lot, Mister!"

Roy smiled, turned, and walked toward the front of the house.

The family arrived at the public cemetery. After Sam retrieved the wreath from the car, they took the short walk to the area where Clara's parents were buried.

"Your wreath really looks nice, Sam," Clara said.

"Yes. They turned out pretty well this year. Lucky I had that cedar. It's easier to make them nice and full. Quay, your oldest brother, is buried nearby, isn't he?"

"Yes, over to the left. He passed on pretty young and barely outlived Mom and Dad. He was gassed in the first war, and he was never in good health after that."

"We'd better be on our way, or we won't have much time to visit Paul and Ethel."

It took only a few minutes to travel from the cemetery to the Franklin Street residence. Shortly thereafter, Jimmie and the four adults sat in the living room to enjoy homemade cookies.

Clara, mentioning their visit to the cemetery, gave information about Grace and her family.

"I'm glad to hear that fellow Grace married seems to have finally landed on his feet," Paul said. "I thought it was a dumb time for them to get married."

"You aren't able to look at things the way young folks do," Ethel observed.

"Maybe so, but sometimes, those young folks need to be able to see past the end of the bedpost."

Jimmie wondered what his uncle meant by that remark and why his father chuckled.

"Let's change the subject," Clara said. "How's your family doing?"

"Bill's a senior in high school this year," Ethel said, "and he'll turn eighteen in April. It sure would be nice to have this war business over soon. Last year, it was like some of the graduates got a diploma in one hand and an induction notice in the other."

"It's hard to keep being patriotic when you think of the cost in terms of all the young people we're losing."

A lull in the conversation gave Jimmie a chance to relate the experience of giving a serviceman a ride and proudly showed the shoulder patch. Sam detailed the young man's description of his military experience and new assignment.

"Nice to know something good came out of Bucktown," Paul said, making Ethel frown and shake her head.

"What do you hear from Edna?" Clara asked. "Is she still in Hawaii?"

"Yes. We hear from her on a pretty regular basis. She's very busy. She had a terrible time during the days after the sneak attack on Pearl Harbor. That was followed by a lull for a couple months, but after the island hopping started, they're getting a steady load of wounded coming back. She got a promotion last month from Lieutenant JG to full Lieutenant. We really miss her, but we're very proud."

"How about you, Paul?" Sam asked. "Is business holding up at the station?"

"We're gettin' by, but everything I sell is on the ration list—gas, oil, and recaps. Most folks think the wartime speed limit is to save gasoline, when, in fact, it's due to the rubber shortage and to save wear and tear on tires. The worst part is the paperwork. God forbid if the ration stamps don't add up with the products listed. Makes you feel like you're part of the fifth column."

They talked for almost an hour.

"Will you folks stay and have a bite of supper with us?" Ethel asked.

"It's nice of you to ask," Clara said, "but I'm sure Sam wants to get on the road. Those old cows have to be milked morning and night no matter what."

Shortly thereafter, they exchanged wishes for a merry Christmas, and the Minor family headed home.

Eight

It was a cold, crisp December morning as Sam and Reed pulled out of the lane onto the hard road. It was their usual weekday trip to the high school, where Sam taught science, and Reed was in the sophomore class. The misty rain and sleet that fell overnight covered everything with an icy glaze.

"Gee, Dad, the sun coming up really reflects on the ice. It's quite a sight."

"Yes, it is, but I have to be careful on the road. I don't want to end up in the ditch."

"Did you call the principal to see if school will be open?"

"No. I didn't think it was necessary. In the six years I've been teaching there, school was canceled only once. Most of the kids are within walking distance. There are only a few students like you who come from the country. Several are out near Eighty-Four."

Sam turned on the car radio, and they soon heard popular music followed by news. Reed wasn't paying attention until he heard a word of interest.

"What was that about some education organization?"

Sam chuckled. "It's probably nothing. It was the Pennsylvania State Education Association, an organization of teachers. They had their annual convention in Harrisburg and passed a resolution that minimum salaries for teachers should be increased from $1,000 to $1,600. Fat chance.

"I'm going to tell you something you have to keep to yourself," Sam said. "Your mother is the only other person who knows.

Next school year, I'm leaving my present job and will move to the city high school. They pay's a little better, and I'll have a lighter teaching load. I'll teach only chemistry and physics. There'll be no more biology and general science."

"That's quite a shock. That means I won't have you for chemistry next year."

"That might not be a bad thing. It could be uncomfortable. If you got good grades, people might think I wasn't being fair. Anyway, it's a good idea to be set pretty solid in your job when the war ends, and the guys start coming home. There are bound to be changes.

"Like I said, keep that to yourself. I told Mr. Westlake, the principal, so he can start looking for a replacement. Anyway, we're almost in Prosperity. Dave Conger called last night to ask for a lift into town."

"What's that about?"

"He retired from Specialty Glass the year before the war started. He was their top guy for making precision lenses for telescopes and other gadgets. They also have government contracts for some secret stuff, maybe weapons systems. The company calls him in from time-to-time. I'm guessing it's for the final meticulous work or maybe to train people. Since it's secret work, don't embarrass him by asking about it."

They stopped, and Dave sat in the car.

"I sure appreciate you giving me a lift into town," Dave said.

"Glad to help," Sam said.

"They seem to be able to offer me a few days' work each month. My pension doesn't amount to much, so this helps."

He looked out the window. "That'll probably dry up after the war ends. That radar stuff is OK for locating things at long distance, but up closer, you need to be able to see things, no matter if it's underwater or high in the air."

Reed glanced at his father without comment.

They drove into Washington. The sun was up by then, and the ice on the trees began to melt and fall. The few cars on the road into town were able to maintain a better speed, though they didn't exceed the wartime limit of thirty-five.

Parking at the rear of the building, they went inside. Sam walked toward his classroom, while Reed was among the handful of students already there. The rest wouldn't arrive for another twenty minutes.

As he sometimes did, Reed stopped to look at the exhibit in one of the glass-enclosed trophy cases in the foyer labeled *Our Heroes*. It showed pictures of graduates serving in the military, with their names, the years they graduated, and their branches of service. Of the nineteen so honored, most graduated in the mid to late 1930s, with a few dating as far back as the late 1920s, including one who was a Commander in the Navy. The only female was a 1936 graduate who served as an Army nurse. Two fellows Reed vaguely remembered graduated the previous June and were in the Army.

His eyes were drawn to the only picture edged in black, a 1937 graduate named Louis Celenni, an Army Air Force fighter pilot killed in 1943. He remembered the memorial service held at the school the previous year. It had a patriotic flare, though it was understandably somber. He recalled Louis' younger sister sobbing throughout the event.

From there, Red walked to the gym and ran the large dust mop up and down the floor. His pact with the janitor allowed him to shoot baskets until first period in return for doing that
chore.

By late morning, after third period, Sam had free time and went to the furnace room in the basement level for a cigarette. It was always warm there, and he caught a dusty, smoky smell. The furniture consisted of a few nondescript chairs and small table in addition to a damaged teacher's desk that somehow escaped being discarded and was given to the janitor.

As he entered the furnace room, Sam passed Art Erickson, the shop teacher, on his way out.

"Any of your young fellows lose fingers this morning?" Sam asked, grinning.

"No. We've been lucky so far." Art smiled. "I wanted to thank you again for the blood from the butchering. Anna's busy today making sausages, or *blodkorv,* as they're called in the old country. I'm licking my chops thinking about a good, old-fashioned Swedish dinner tonight."

"You're very welcome. If not for you, it would have spilled over the ground."

"If there's anything I can do for you, let me know."

"Maybe there is. I sent away for plans to build a hutch cabinet, and I have more than enough rough-cut cherry. After the first of the year, I'd like to bring those in to go over with you and see how I should start."

"Sounds good. Bring a piece of the cherry with you, and we'll see how it planes up."

Sam settled into a chair as Art left and lit a cigarette. As he exhaled, he picked up the day's Pittsburgh newspaper and perused the front page. The hall door opened, and the math teacher, Vincent Peroni, came in.

"Greetings, Vinney. How's your morning going?"

"The worst is over now that the general math class is done." He shook his head in resignation and disgust. "I know most of the kids hate mathematics, but I can't imagine how they got out of grade school. So much for that. What's in the news?"

"Nothing much about the war. Everything seems to be moving favorably in the Philippines and in Europe. Here's something unexpected. One of the Congressional Committees is holding hearings to look into why we were caught off guard at Pearl Harbor. It must have to do with the anniversary coming up. It smells like politics to me."

As Vinney sat and lit a cigarette, Sam studied the newspaper.

"Here's a surprise," Sam said. "Roosevelt may start easing some of the restrictions on the internment of Japanese in the western states. This article says some of them may be permitted to return to their homes. That's interesting, don't you think?"

"Hmmm." Vinney rubbed his chin, staring into space.

"That strikes me as a thoughtful nonanswer. Care to fill in the blanks for me?"

Vinney hesitated. "Sam, what I'm going to tell you is something I haven't shared with anyone outside my immediate family. You're probably not aware that the concern over spies and espionage in the aftermath of Pearl Harbor wasn't just confined to the Japanese. Sure, that's where the emphasis and publicity were, but the government was also worried about the Germans and Italians who still had ties to the old country. There was anxiety, perhaps justified, that there could be damage to facilities that would hamper our war effort. Some of those people are interned, too.

"I was sitting at home one night in February, 1942, when there was a knock at the door. Two men who identified themselves as FBI agents showed me their credentials. What followed was the most-uncomfortable hour and a half of my life."

"Good Lord!" Sam said. "Did they accuse you of being a spy?"

"Not directly, but I could tell that was what they were looking for. They knew when my parents came over from the old country and when they gained their citizenship. They started by asking about any relatives in the old country and if I were in contact with them. They showed me a list of organizations, but I'd heard of only a couple. They asked if I belonged to any of them or knew anyone who did. Did I spend any time around the steel mill in Canton Township? Some of the questions were almost like trick questions, like the old joke about, 'When did you stop beating your wife?'"

"How did it end?"

"Finally, after an hour and a half, the one who seemed to be in charge folded up his papers, put them into his briefcase, and nodded.

He said they didn't have any more questions and thanked me for my cooperation. They'd be in touch if anything else came up. It's been almost two years, and that hasn't happened, thank the Lord."

Vinney and Sam were silent.

"I think it's terrible that they came after you," Sam finally said. "You're as patriotic as anyone I know."

"That's right. I was pretty bitter afterward, and I still am to some extent. I don't know if I ever told you, but my father was, of course, an alien. When the last war began, he was drafted. He did his duty, served, and when he was discharged, he gained his citizenship. It rubbed me the wrong way to have our patriotism questioned."

He shook his head. "If you recall, right after Pearl Harbor, our armed forces were next to nothing, and there was a lot of anxiety that we might be invaded on the West Coast. Back in the thirties, when a lot of people were hurt financially, some of those extreme political ideas took root. There was the German-American Bund, and…what was the other outfit? Oh, yeah. They were the Silver Shirts. They didn't call themselves fascists, but it was pretty clear where they stood.

"I don't know, Sam. It's becoming clear that a lot of loyal, patriotic Americans were locked up. That experience scared the shit out of me. Sometimes, when the powers-that-be are faced with a touchy issue, they overreact. I guess that's what happened, but that doesn't make it right."

"It sure doesn't. Oops. There goes the bell for the next period. We have to go. That was quite an experience you had. I appreciate your confidence in sharing it with me. Rest assured, I'll keep it to myself."

The school day continued its routine and ended at mid-afternoon. Most students left the building quickly. The teachers stayed for another half an hour, which meant Reed had to wait for Sam. Some days, he spent the time in study hall to work on pressing homework assignments. That day wasn't the case, so Reed went to the gym to watch basketball practice, where he joined a few other students and the parents of some of the players.

He sat beside Mark Parsons, a classmate.

"Waiting until your dad's ready to go?" Mark asked.

"That's about it. I'll kill some time and see how the guys are improving in their figure-eight drill."

"I'd say they're looking pretty good. I'm surprised you didn't go out for basketball. You did really well on the football team. You were the only sophomore on the starting lineup."

"That was a different story. In football, all freshmen started out as rookies with no prior experience. The town kids were brought out from their grade school for gym and played basketball in the seventh and eighth grades. They're way ahead of us hicks from the sticks, and I knew I couldn't catch up."

"I believe they've got a game tomorrow night. Who are they playing?"

"It's with Burgettstown. It'll be a tough game. At least, they were good last year. Did you hear of anyone who's going to the game?"

"No."

"That figures. It's pretty early in the month to use gas-rationing stamps for unnecessary travel."

Reed looked for his father, as the practice continued, and he soon saw Sam at the hallway door. "There's Dad. See you tomorrow, Mark." He stood to leave.

"See you."

Outside, as they walked to the car, Sam handed Reed the keys. "Looks like there's no ice or snow anymore. You might as well take the wheel, and maybe I can sleep a bit on the way home."

Nine

The kitchen door opened, and Sam, accompanied by a rush of cold air, stepped in from the outside, set down two milk buckets on the floor, and rubbed his hands briskly.

"It's good to get in out of the cold," he said, seeing Jimmie and Reed eating breakfast. "Looks like you guys are about finished. We'll be able to get an early start for the big trip to Pittsburgh. Where's your mom?"

"She went back upstairs," Reed said. "I think she's changing clothes."

"I'd better do the same. I can't tromp into those fancy department stores with cow shit on my shoes. We'll be on our way soon. Reed, once you finish eating, I'd like you to start the Ford, so it can warm up."

"OK, Dad."

The family was soon in the car, driving toward a shopping adventure in Pittsburgh. It was a crisp day with high clouds and no snow in the forecast.

"How long will it take us to get to Pittsburgh, Dad?" Jimmie asked.

"I'd usually plan for an hour, but the question this time of year is the traffic. Christmas shopping means a lot of extra cars on the road, so we could get tied up. We'll have to wait and see."

"Gee, Dad. An hour seems like a long time."

"It'll pass quicker than you think. After we're past Washington, there'll be plenty of things to look at you haven't seen before."

Jimmie found it difficult to be relaxed and patient. It was five years since their last trip to Pittsburgh, and his recollection of that excursion, which included a visit to the Allegheny County Fair, was vague and incomplete.

That's where I got my piggy bank, he remembered. *Dad looked at the bottom and said the pottery was made in Czechoslovakia. He told me to take good care of it, because Germany took over that country, so it no longer existed.*

I remember a machine that took pictures of people walking by. You could see them on a little movie screen. It was called tele...something.

His attempts to sit still were frustrated by glimpses of the passing landscape, making him twist and partially stand for a better view. Reed sat on the other side of the rear seat, leaning back with his eyes closed, apparently resting and thinking about the day.

I hope I don't have to stand around for hours while Mom looks at all the clothes, Reed thought. *I wouldn't mind looking through the sporting goods and maybe at some books. Dad said we might be able to slip away from the department store and walk to the old Fort Pitt blockhouse. He thinks they've got old guns and other stuff to see.*

As Sam predicted, once they were through Washington and on the main road to Pittsburgh, the countryside became unfamiliar, and there were new things to see. One large intrusion in the rural landscape caught Jimmie's eye.

"Dad, what's that building on your side?" he asked. "There are smaller buildings near it."

"That's a place you definitely want to avoid. That's Morganza."

"What is it?"

"It's a reform school for kids and young people who get into trouble with the law. It's like a jail and isn't a nice place to be."

"A jail? What things did people do to be put in there?"

Sam paused and grinned at Clara. "Not brushing their teeth, talking sass to their parents, that sort of thing."

"Sam, don't tease the boy," Clara admonished.

"No, Jimmie. Young folks get put there for doing serious things like stealing, hurting people, destroying property, and that sort of thing."

Jimmie was quiet and reflective for several minutes. The conversation alerted Reed, though, and he began studying the landscape, too.

"Look at all the smoke to the left, Dad. Is something on fire?" Reed asked.

"That's about where Bridgehead is located. I heard they re-opened several old beehive coke ovens over there. It's probably smoke from that."

"I don't understand. What's that about?'

"It's part of the war effort. Coke is coal that's been heated or burned off to drive out the impurities. What's left is almost pure carbon, and it burns very hot, which is required for making steel. Several years ago, they found if they made coke in a controlled environment in something called a by-product oven, they could capture the smoke you're seeing and make useful things from it."

"Like what?"

"Oh, tars and gasses that can be refined to make solvents, medicines, and plastics."

"So why use the old beehive ovens?"

"The war increased our need for steel. The mills operate around the clock seven days a week. The need for coke has skyrocketed, and that's the only way to quickly meet the demand."

"I wouldn't want to live near all that smoke."

"No. It can't be very healthy. Hopefully, the war will be over in the next year or so, so they won't have to keep the ovens going. The smoke's another sacrifice we have to make as part of the war effort."

They began to see the transition from a rural landscape to a more built-up environment. Individual homes and occasional commercial buildings replaced farm buildings and fields of livestock.

A few miles later, the change to a totally urban environment became complete, with the roadway continuously lined by structures on both sides.

"Are we almost there?" Jimmie asked.

"We're getting there. Just beyond that curve up ahead, we'll go down a grade into the Liberty Tubes. When we come out the other side, we'll go across the Monongahela River, and then we'll be there."

"Tubes? That's a tunnel, isn't it?"

"That's right, but it's short. We'll be through in a minute or so if the traffic isn't tied up."

As Sam predicted, they drove quickly through the tunnel and onto the bridge across the river. Ahead, they saw the multistory buildings of Pittsburgh's downtown.

"Look!" Jimmie said. "There's a big boat on the river pushing something in front of it."

"Those are barges full of coal or coke," Sam explained, "headed for a steel mill or power plant. There's always plenty of activity on the river these days."

They soon crossed the bridge and turned left onto the first cross street to head toward the shopping district.

"I'm assuming your preferred destination is Kauffmanns," Sam told Clara.

"Yes," she replied. "I've always liked their selections, and it's only a few blocks to walk to Hornes or Gimbels."

"All right. There's a couple of parking lots within a short walk of Kauffmanns, so I'll try for them."

There was much to see, as Sam drove down the streets. The boys and their mother made note of the various stores and office buildings. Many had decorations heralding the holiday season. They observed trolleys and buses on the wider streets. A few street peddlers stood around, and Salvation Army workers ringing bells on corners had baskets for donations.

"It looks foggy or hazy, Dad," Reed said. "It's strange so many cars have their headlights on during the day."

"That isn't fog or natural haze. The air's polluted with smoke and grit from the steel mills and other factories up and down the riverbanks. It gets trapped in the valleys here until the wind or the temperature changes. It comes and goes, so they leave their lights on all the time."

Sam slowed almost to a stop. "We're in luck. There are some vacant spots in this parking lot."

Once the car was parked, the family walked toward the department store. The sidewalks were crowded with businessmen, young people Reed and Jimmie's ages, shoppers carrying bundles and packages, and men in military uniforms. Lighted traffic signals stood at nearly every intersection. On major streets, policemen provided additional safety for the movement of vehicles and pedestrians.

As they approached the department store, they saw the street-level windows.

"Look, Mom!" Jimmie said. "See all the toys?"

"Indeed. That's quite a show."

They stopped and tried to find a vantage point among the other onlookers to view the displays. The windows were well laid out, and the center area featured a toy village with a Lionel train running around the perimeter. On one side was a variety of sports equipment, including skis, balls and bats for baseball or softball, ice skates, and a football. At the other end were goods for scholarly young people, including books and school supplies. A selection of dolls sat near the front of the display.

They moved to the next window and saw a festively decorated sign proclaiming *Santa's Workshop*. A crowd six people deep stood close to the window, blocking the family's view. Sam was the only one tall enough to see over the heads in front. He squatted down and motioned Jimmie closer.

"Hop on my shoulders. You have to see this."

He got on Sam's shoulders, then looked, as Sam stood.

"Wow! It's a bunch of elves making toys!"

I have to admit this is well done, Sam thought. *Those elves must be skinny, preteen girls in green outfits. The hats with the fake pointy ears are a clever touch. They're pretending to make a sled. In that other area is a small doll factory. The big chair must be for Santa, but it's empty. Guess he went out for a smoke or a beer.*

Sam smiled. "OK, Jimmie. You'd better get down. It's cold out here. I'm sure your mom wants to get inside."

They moved down the sidewalk and through the revolving doors into the department store. The transition from cold into the warm interior was enhanced by the combined aromas of perfumes, cologne, and powders.

"Oh, my!" Jimmie said. "What smells so good?"

"It's stuff women like to use," Sam said. "It's at the counters on your right."

"I'd have to say it's better than what a cow stable smells like," Reed said.

Clara frowned. "We don't need to let everyone know we're a bunch of farmers." She rummaged in her pocketbook and took out a piece of note paper. "Men's clothing and sporting goods are on the third floor. Let's take the escalator straight ahead and see what we can find up there."

Jimmie had some trouble getting his feet on the moving plates properly. Once on the third floor, the family separated. Sam and Reed went to look at sporting goods, while Clara and Jimmie sought men's clothing. She wanted to buy dress pants for Sam. Jimmie tried to be patient, while Clara thoroughly looked through the possibilities.

She finally made her selection, and Jimmie watched with interest, as the clerk wrote something on a pad, tore off a sheet, and folded it with the money Clara gave him. Those were placed in a small, round, metal container the size of a sweet potato, which he placed in an opening in a pipe attached to the desk. With a strange sucking sound, the container disappeared.

A few moments later, the container returned from another pipe and dropped into a wire basket. The clerk opened it, extracted the contents, and handed Clara her receipt and change.

Jimmie was too shy to ask about the procedure in front of the clerk, but the moment they left the counter, he asked, "Mom, how do they do that? Why not have a cash register right at the counter and make change like Mr. Fulton does at the store?"

"I don't know how the system works. It's some kind of vacuum thing. Try to remember to ask your father. He might know. It must be more efficient than having cash registers and money all over the place."

Clara and Jimmie walked across the floor and found Sam and Reed waiting for them at the escalators.

"Did you men find anything interesting?" she asked.

"Not really," Sam said. "We wandered through the hardware and sporting goods, but there wasn't anything I couldn't live without."

Clara nodded. "Jimmie and I will spend some time on the upper floors. I want to look at the women's clothing, not that I plan to buy anything, but I might see something in giftware to be presents for Marge or Gayle."

"Reed and I'll go out to explore the city a bit. He's never seen the blockhouse at old Fort Pitt, and we might wander through the market and get a sandwich at the Oyster House."

"That sounds like a good idea. Noon will be here soon. Jimmie and I can find something to eat at the restaurant on the top floor."

Sam paused and rubbed his chin, a sign he was considering something. "Clara, we ought to try to head for home around three o'clock. That'll get us home by four and time to get the cows in and start milking before dark."

"That should give me enough time. I plan to go to Horne's before we leave. There's a little coffee shop on the mezzanine. Let's plan to meet there."

Jimmie found it tiring and boring, accompanying his mother to various store sections. Twice, she told him to sit in a waiting area, while she ventured to nearby parts of the store. The last time, she returned with a shopping bag full of items.

"I don't know about you," she said, "but I'm almost tuckered out and ready for a break. Let's go to the restaurant back there and have lunch."

"Sounds great to me, Mom."

He had almost no experience eating at a restaurant. *This will be different from when Dad takes Reed and me into the Coney Island Lunch for a hotdog,* he thought.

A lady greeted them at the entrance, carrying several menus, and led them to a table. As they were seated, she handed Clara one of the menus.

"Would you like a children's menu, Madam?"

"Yes, we would."

"Jimmie, look through this and see if there's anything you might like."

He studied the menu. "Mom, these meals have toy names, like Jump Rope, Pick-Up Sticks, and such. This one looks good. It's the Teddy Bear, and it has my favorite, applesauce."

"That's a good choice." Clara, who had already lit a cigarette, inhaled smoke and nodded. "It includes vegetable soup and a grilled cheese sandwich. We'll order that for you."

The waitress brought their food on a tray and placed it before them. Clara picked up her fork and was ready to start eating when she saw Jimmie frown.

"Is something wrong?" she asked.

"Gee whiz, Mom. Look at this tiny dish of applesauce. I'll bet it's not even two spoonfuls. It's hardly a smell."

She smiled. "That's pretty skimpy. All I can say is, eating in a restaurant isn't like at home. You'll have to make up for it when we're back."

Clara finished first and had coffee and another cigarette, while Jimmie completed his meal.

When Sam and Reed reached the first floor of the department store, Sam saw a chance to do some Christmas shopping.

"Reed, let's stop in the cosmetics area," he said. "Maybe I can find something your mother might like."

They walked to a counter and were immediately approached by a clerk.

"Can I help you gentlemen with anything?"

She was an attractive, well-dressed, mature woman. Sam felt she would be more help than any of the young kids hired for the season.

"Yes, perhaps you can," Sam said. "I need to get something for my wife but have nothing in mind."

She smiled. "You aren't alone. I hear that frequently. We're right by the lipsticks, and we have a wide variety of shades. What color does she use?"

"She doesn't use lipstick. Other than powder and a little light rouge on her cheeks, she doesn't put anything on her face."

"How about perfume or cologne?"

"That's a possibility, but nothing too strong. She wouldn't like that."

The woman nodded. "I have some items over here that would fill the bill."

As they approached the counter, the clerk pointed out some colognes. "Each of these are two dollars. The perfumes on the lower shelf are a little more."

Sam tried the various fragrances to make his selection. Reed, who thought of his father as only masculine, found the process strange, if not amusing.

A few minutes later, their purchase concluded, Sam and Reed left the store.

The walk to the historic site took less than fifteen minutes, which may have seemed longer, since the temperature had risen only slightly, and a stiff breeze started. As they neared their destination along the Monongahela River, the cold became more intense.

Reed was only moderately impressed by the blockhouse and artifacts it contained. There were antique firearms and accessories, including powder horns and bullet molds, but he'd seen similar things at home. He studied the papers in a display case and a map that purported to show the importance of the three rivers location during the French and Indian War. It took Reed and Sam only thirty minutes to look at all the materials.

"Where are we headed now, Dad?" Reed asked, as they left.

"I'm getting hungry, so I'd like to go to the market area where I know we can get something good."

"You mentioned the Oyster House. What's that?"

"It's a pretty interesting place. It's a restaurant and bar that's been around almost a hundred years. It's not fancy, but you can look at the clientele and see a cross section of society. You'll see folks in raggedy clothes who look like they don't know where their next meal will come from, and standing or sitting beside them will be fellows in hundred-dollar suits who are probably doctors and lawyers. The food's not bad, either." He chuckled.

Their route took them away from the dampness of the river. They entered sections with taller buildings that helped block the wind, which made for a more-temperate walk. Reed looked at the stores and places of business they passed.

Looking ahead, he saw a theater with a distinctive marquee emblazoned with the words *Girls, Girls, Girls*. Below that in smaller letters, he read *Continuous Shows*. As they walked closer, he saw large posters showing scantily clad women in provocative poses. A large banner proclaimed, *Men in Uniform Half Price*.

As they approached the front door, Reed looked in the adjacent alley and saw two women standing there in bathrobes, smoking cigarettes. One saw him staring and opened her robe to reveal she was wearing something like a bathing suit.

"Come on in, Honey," she said, "and I'll show you a whole lot more."

Reed quickly averted his eyes. They walked on, and he was grateful for the cold wind on his warm face.

"What in the world was that about?" he asked finally.

Sam grinned. "That was a burlesque theater. Those shows are about all that's left of vaudeville. It mostly involved women, whose primary skill is taking off as much clothing as allowed in whatever city they're performing in. It's done to music. There may be a man or two in the acts, and their role is to make off-color remarks and jokes."

Reed considered that. Only one of several questions that came to mind was something he felt comfortable asking.

"I've heard the word vaudeville, but I'm not sure what it means."

"Back in the twenties, vaudeville was a major source of entertainment in most cities for ordinary people. The theaters provided reasonable admission prices for what you'd call a variety show. There were singers, dancers, comedians, and jugglers. You'd see skits, normally comedies, but sometimes they were more dramatic.

"Those entertainers traveled from city to city to put on shows. Some of the more accomplished made it into the big time in major cities like New York, Chicago, and San Francisco. By the early thirties, however, vaudeville couldn't compete with radio and the movies, so it died. It was an important step in the growth of the entertainment world. Several of today's top performers in the movies and on radio got started in vaudeville."

Sam looked ahead. "So much for the daily lecture. Here we are at the Oyster House."

As they entered the establishment, Reed was surprised by its size. He expected a larger place. The bar extended the length of the room on one side, and a row of tables sat along the other with varied types of customers, rich and not so rich, as Sam explained. There were also several young men in military uniforms. The place was crowded, but Sam found a small, unoccupied table.

"Looks like the lunchtime crowd is thinning out," Sam said. "If we came earlier, we'd have had a hard time finding a place to sit down."

"I don't see a kitchen or door leading to one. I thought you said we'd get something to eat here."

"Oh, we can. Look at the far wall to the right of the cash register. See that little door? That opens to a dumb waiter. The food comes down on a hand-powered elevator from the kitchen upstairs."

Just as Sam spoke, a worker behind the bar walked to the door, opened it, and removed a food tray. He distributed the servings to the customers seated and standing at the bar, then he took some to a couple at one of the tables.

Sam placed their order, and soon, the food was served.

"Holy cow, Dad," Reed exclaimed. "I never saw a sandwich this big!"

"That's their specialty. Those are big buns, but there's as much fish hanging out the sides as there is inside."

"What are those round things people at the next table are eating? They're as big as a baseball."

Sam chuckled. "Maybe not quite that big, but they're large. Those are oysters, or at least somewhere in all that dough and crumbs there is one. I never had a taste for those, but a lot of folks do, because they sell plenty of them."

There was no conversation between Reed and Sam for the next several minutes, as they devoured their sandwiches. When they finished, they sipped their drinks, savoring their repast.

"You seem to know a lot about Pittsburgh, Dad. How come?"

"I wouldn't say I know a lot. It's a big city. Back in the twenties when I was in college, some of my fraternity brothers and I came over for an evening or a weekend. We might see a vaudeville show, or there might be a football or basketball game at Pitt or one of the other colleges. Our fraternity had a chapter at Pitt, and we could stay there for free. Those were some of my good old days," he said with a smile, resting his chin on his hand and staring into space.

After a moment, Sam glanced at his watch. "We'd better head out of here and go toward Hornes. Before you know it, your mom and Jimmie will be there, waiting for us."

They arrived first, and Sam and Reed went to the mezzanine coffee shop.

"I guess I'll have some coffee," Sam said. "You probably want a bottle of pop."

They sat for only a few minutes before Clara and Jimmie arrived. The family stayed a little longer, then walked to their car. Their departure time was ahead of the afternoon rush hour, so they made it across the river and through the Liberty Tubes quickly.

They were past the suburbs and into the rural countryside when there was a loud noise, similar to hitting a pothole, and a series of thumps. Sam slowed the car and pulled off to the shoulder.

"What was that noise?" Jimmie asked. "Why are we stopping?"

"We just had a flat tire, Dummy," Reed said in disgust.

"Yes, we had a flat tire," Sam said, "but you don't need to call your brother a dummy. Let's get out and fix it. I hope it wasn't a blowout. Most of the tires on this old buggy are more patches than tire. Maybe it's my imagination, but it seems like those synthetic recaps don't hold up like the regular rubber tires we had before the war. I'll need to apply for a certificate for a new tire."

Sam and the boys got out. In a few minutes, they changed the tire and continued driving. All of them were tired by then, so conversation was limited. The day's activities made many of the family pensive.

Clara was only marginally satisfied with her visit to the department stores. *I was sure I'd find something for Marge and Gayle,* she thought. *Maybe I'll find something in Washington.*

Jimmie had been impressed by the Christmas displays in the store windows. *Wouldn't it be neat if there was a Santa Claus, and he had workshops with elves making toys?*

Sam was relieved to have finished his Christmas shopping. *I'm pretty sure she'll like that perfume.*

Of all the family, Reed had the most to think about. Walking past the burlesque show was uppermost in his mind. *I wonder how much of their clothing they take off during the shows? Do they really get completely naked? I can't believe how big the sandwiches were at the Oyster House. Dad surprised me with the things he told me today. I guess he thinks I'm becoming a man.*

By the time they reached the familiar territory of Washington, snow was falling. As they traveled the last few miles to home, snow accumulated on the road. Sam slowed the car, and gravel rattled under the fenders, as they pulled into the lane.

The family was home, ready to be thrust into the routine of their customary chores and pursuits.

Ten

I'd better check the temperature on the candy, so I don't spoil the batch, Clara thought. *I was lucky Frank had some sugar stamps someone else couldn't use.* Peering into the liquid bubbling in the heavy saucepan, she studied the thermometer. *Only a few degrees to go. Time to add the green coloring and oil of wintergreen.*

She lifted the pan slightly off the burner and gently swirled to mix the contents. She replaced the pan on the burner and nodded a few moments later. *Now it's time for fast hands.*

She poured the thickening material onto the marble top of the adjacent utility cabinet and worked quickly with a spatula and heavy scissors to cut the rapidly hardening material into small pieces. The finished product was warm, hard candy.

With the red cinnamon I made last Wednesday, there's enough for us and some for a couple of little jars for gifts. It's very festive looking.

Jimmie finished playing with his Lincoln Logs under the dining room table and gathered all the pieces, putting them into the box before dragging the box out from under the dining room table. That was his favorite place to build cabins and forts to ward off enemy attacks. As he savored the thought of his latest victory, his satisfaction was interrupted by his mother's footsteps, as she walked into the dining room from the kitchen.

"Jimmie, were you planning on going up the hollow to cut pine this afternoon?"

"Yes, I was, Mom. It's getting dark earlier each night, and I have less time after school. Dad told me the other night that he had two more orders for me, so I'd better get after it."

"That's a good idea, but it's still early afternoon. I'd like you to run to the store and get a couple things I need."

"Sure, Mom."

"If you're tired from the big trip to Pittsburgh yesterday, it can be put off."

"No, I'm fine. Do you have a list?"

"Yes. Here it is, along with the ration book. Frank will take out whatever stamps he needs. Just don't lose the book. None of these items weigh much, and Jim will put them into a small box or bag for you.

"One other thing. Sometimes, he's able to get some cigarettes, and he'll have a couple packs for us. If he does, don't let anyone else in the store see them. They're just for his regular customers, not the loafers who sit around all day and hardly buy anything."

"Why do you call them loafers?"

"They just sit around there all day and gossip like old women. They never work."

Jimmie grinned. "I guess that *is* a good name for them."

He put on his outside clothing and galoshes. Clara walked to the door with him and handed him the list and ration book.

"Did I hear Dad leave in the car a little while ago?" Jimmie asked.

"Yes. He and Reed went to the church. Reed has some parts in the Christmas program coming up, and they have rehearsal this afternoon. While that's going on, Mr. Cooper asked your dad to make some repairs to the outside entrance door to the basement. Your father can't say no to anyone who asks for help. They'll be back in an hour. You be careful on the wooden steps down to the footbridge. There might be ice on them, and you could take a nasty fall."

"Don't worry, Mom. I'll be fine."

On the other side of the creek, snow was packed on the path across the bottom land and up the grade to the store, but Jimmie saw four or five inches of snow on either side. *If that was packed down, it would be good for sledding,* he thought.

At the top of the grade, he opened the small gate that connected the fence on one side and the small warehouse that was part of the station property on the other. A few more steps took him across the railroad tracks to the storefront.

Entering the general store was always an adventure for Jimmie, with its endless merchandise to look at and wonder about. He saw canned food and bakery products, candy bars and penny candy in a big glass case, a large metal case full of cold water for pop, and another glass case filled with pen knives, Zippo lighters, flashlights, and other goods.

He has work shoes, socks, and work shirts up front, Jimmie thought, *but I've never seen anyone buying that stuff. They must, or he wouldn't have them.*

Jimmie was greeted by a variety of odors, with tobacco smoke the most pervasive. Looking around, he was glad to see there weren't any pipe smokers. That was the worst.

He smelled the oil the owner applied to the plain wooden floor occasionally to absorb the dust, and there was the smell of the coal burning in the pot-bellied stove in the center of the room. The summers weren't too bad, with ventilation provided by the two screen doors.

In the store, he met a woman on her way out carrying basket of groceries.

"Hi, Jimmie. How are you today?"

"I'm OK, Mrs. Ruff."

"That's good. By the way, have your mom and dad had any word about your cousin, Russell?"

"Yes. Mom had a call from Aunt Sarah a few days ago. Russell finished his basic training, and I think they said he has to go to California. Dad said that means he'll fight the Japs, not the Germans."

"Maybe this whole business will be over soon, so he won't have to fight anybody. Say hello to your mom for me. Tell her I'll see her in church on Sunday."

On the wall to the right, just inside the door, Jimmie saw a patriotic poster he hadn't seen before. *They change them sometimes, but this one's really neat. It's about the sixth drive for war bonds. I like how the soldier is pointing with one hand and has his other arm back as if ready to throw a grenade. He looks brave. I've got to get a lot more stamps in my book before it's filled up to get a bond.*

Jimmie walked the length of the store to where the counter with the cash register and scales waited. As he passed the stove, he was greeted, or perhaps he was accosted, by one of the loafers warming his hands, an elderly man named Hap.

"How's everyone doing with the Minor clan these days?"

"OK, I guess."

"Is your peter still growin'?"

The other men laughed, and Jimmie felt his cheeks grow warm. Knowing the question was better left unanswered, he shrugged and continued toward the counter.

Frank, the owner, grinned and reached for the grocery list and ration book. "Don't let them get your goat, Jimmie. They're just tryin' to have a little fun." He studied the list. "I believe I have everything except longhorn cheese. Tell your mom I'll get some on Thursday when I go into town."

He retrieved the items on the list and set them in a small cardboard box. After he took the stamps from the ration book, he scanned the store. Satisfied none of the other customers were watching, he reached below the counter and set something in a small paper bag, which he placed in the box, winking at Jimmie.

I suppose that's the cigarettes, Jimmie thought.

"Almost forgot," Frank said. "I've got something for you folks for Christmas."

From the back of the counter, Frank produced a box that Jimmie recognized from the previous year—pecan brittle. Frank said it came from somewhere in Georgia. Jimmie thought it tasted pretty good.

Thanking Frank, he carried the box of groceries from the store. *That's the first Christmas present of the year,* he thought.

Outside, he prepared to retrace his steps toward home when he heard excited voices behind the warehouse. He hurried over. As he reached the gate, he saw four of his schoolmates in the field below.

"Hey!" Jimmie called. "What are you guys up to?"

"We're building a snow slide and jump," Jerry Hickman said.

They packed down the snow and piled more over boards to serve as a jump.

"That looks pretty good. Looks like you're about finished and ready to try it out."

"Yep. Why don't you get your Yankee Jumper and try it with us?"

"I'm afraid not. I have to take these things from the store back home, then I have to cut pine to sell to some of the teachers where Dad works. Besides, I don't want to risk my Yankee Jumper on that jump. I broke the wooden part of a runner last year doing that, and Dad had to fix it. I'll see you at school tomorrow."

Less than half an hour later, Jimmie was heading up the hollow past the barn and pulled his sled behind him. On it sat a large cardboard box with lengths of binder twine and a small handsaw. Because of the snowfall two days earlier, it wasn't an easy trip. The route was little more than a wide path used by the tractor and wagon or other farm equipment.

With a boxful of pine braches, coming back won't be easy, he realized. *I'll have to be careful and go slow, or the whole thing will tip over.*

He reached the end of the trail, where it merged into a hayfield. *I'll have to cross to the other side of the hollow where Dad planted evergreens several years ago, but that shouldn't be a problem. There wasn't been any water in that little stream for a couple months.*

He easily reached the other side and pulled the sled up the slight grade to the plot where the evergreens stood. They made a distinct change from the surrounding trees and brush that were devoid of leaves. Sam planted them in regular rows with even spacing. The result was that the limbs of adjacent trees overlapped, and the snow didn't reach the ground, which was covered by a brown layer of pine needles.

Dad says cutting the lower limbs off doesn't hurt the trees and makes them grow better. I guess he's right. They seem pretty healthy.

Jimmie started work with the hand saw. In a quarter of an hour, he accumulated a large pile of pine boughs. *That looks like more than enough for two nice bundles. I'd better sort them out and tie them, so if the sled tips over on the way back, gathering them won't be too bad.*

By the time all the limbs were secured in the box on the sled, Jimmie felt the temperature dropping. The sun was low in the west, but there was plenty of daylight for him to retrace his route. As he squatted to grasp the rope and pull the sled, he heard a sound to his left below the pine-tree plot. He looked up in surprise to see a deer coming into view. The animal stopped and looked at him, then Jimmie's foot slipped, and he fell backward. The deer whirled and was gone.

"Wow!" He'd never seen a deer up that close. He couldn't wait to tell Dad and Reed.

He stood and pulled the sled toward the spot where he saw the deer. There were tracks from the deer in the snow, but the deer hadn't returned.

I'd better head for home.

When Jimmie returned and unloaded pine limbs from the sled, the car with Reed and Sam pulled into the lane. As the two got out of the car, Sam looked at the pine limbs and nodded.

"Those are nice, full bundles," Sam said. "The ladies will be more than satisfied."

"You'll never believe what I saw up by the pine trees."

"Then you'd better tell me."

"A deer, and it came only a few feet away and looked at me." He described the event.

"When the deer saw you, it couldn't decide if you were a bush or whatever. When you moved, that was his clue to get out of there."

He paused. "I saw one at a distance back in October when I was cutting corn. With the trees getting more size in the mountains to the east, there's less brush and winter browse for the deer, so they're moving into our area. We may see more."

"Did it have horns?" Reed asked.

He stopped and thought. "No."

"Guess it was a female, a doe."

Sam looked toward the west. "The sun will set soon. Time to get the cows in and the milking done."

Eleven

The snow on the roadway was packed solid. With tire chains, Sam was able to drive at only slightly less-than-normal speed.

"Looks like we'll be able to get into town before noon," Sam said, "as long as we don't get hung up by some fool crossways in the road. It's a good thing we didn't get any more than we had yesterday. I heard on the radio they got fifteen inches in Pittsburgh, and it's a hell of a mess."

"No need to try to break any speed records," Clara said. "There's nothing magic about twelve o'clock. We don't have to be at the doctor's office until one for Jimmie's appointment, and I don't think it'll take long. We'll have all afternoon for shopping after that. You don't have to be home for milking until four or five."

Sam nodded. "I hope Doc can give you something to clear up Jimmie's problem. It seems like that chest cold and sore throat have hung on long enough."

"That's what I hope, too. We should count our lucky stars Dr. Weiss is still around. He's good."

"I agree. He's getting long in the tooth, but he knows his stuff. So many doctors were pulled into the military, but that's where they're needed.'

Clara looked behind her into the back seat. "You guys OK back there?"

"I'm fine," Jimmie said.

"Me, too," Reed said, "as long as I don't choke to death on that cigarette smoke."

"I'll open a window to vent for a bit. That'll take it out."

Reed and Jimmie saw their father studying them in the rear-view mirror. By his stern expression, it was clear that Reed overstepped his bounds by criticizing his mother. The boys slumped into the back seat without any further words.

Three miles later, they approached the first stream that was crossed by a covered bridge. It was a noisy experience, with the sound of the snow chains and the roar of the engine amplified in the confined area.

As they left the bridge, Clara said, "I'm always glad when we get through one of those things. I don't think they're safe."

"You may have a point," Sam said. "They're made of wood, which can rot, but they're inspected pretty often."

"I suppose, but they're so old. You'd think someone would build a proper bridge of steel and concrete."

"I'm sure they will, but it won't be until after the war. That's where all the money's going. After I'm dead and gone, you'll be hard pressed to find a covered bridge anywhere except in picture books, as a sign of bygone times."

A few miles farther down the road, the tires made different sounds. The chain-covered tires bit into the packed snow and crunched, followed by a rattle of the chains against the hard road surface. Jimmie stood partially erect and looked back to see that some patches of road were almost bare of snow.

"It must not have snowed that much up this way, Dad," he said.

"I think it probably did. It's just that the closer to town we get, the more traffic has been on the road, and that wears off the snow. What you've noticed will give us a few minutes' delay. I have to pull off here by Harold Weir's lane and take off the chains. Driving on bare road will wear them to bits. It's not good for the tires, either. I don't want to get these recapped any sooner than I have to."

Sam stopped and got out. Reed pushed forward in the seat to follow him.

"You stay put, Jimmie," Clara said. "No point you getting out there and taking a chill. It won't take long, anyway."

She was right. A few minutes later, the chains were off and in the trunk.

As they continued down the road, Jimmie saw something new. "Look! The whole end of that barn is painted with a Mail Pouch sign. I don't think I saw that before. It must've just happened."

"Not really," Sam said. "I first noticed that toward the end of October before it started to get cold. It could be we haven't been by here since."

"It looks nice, better than just those old plain boards. It says, *Treat Yourself to the Best.*"

Clara gave a derisive sound. "Hmph! Chewing tobacco! Some treat—if you want bad breath and broken teeth. I can't imagine it would be very healthy for your mouth and throat, either. I sure hope none of you take up that disgusting habit."

Sam chuckled. "I can't argue with that, but it's a good way of getting the end of the barn painted without costing anything. It's a new form of advertising for motorists, too."

"Kinda like the Burma Shave signs on Route 19 near Amity?" Reed asked.

"Yes, pretty much."

"Why don't they have Burma Shave signs on this road?" Jimmie asked.

"I guess Route 19 has more traffic, and they probably only put them where they think the most people will see them."

Soon, they bumped over the railroad tracks at the bottom of the Main Street hill and proceeded toward the business district. Jimmie eagerly anticipated shopping trips to town. His interest and excitement increased, as they went down the street.

Not much has changed since the last time, Jimmie thought. *There's the big supermarket. I hope we go in there before we go home. It always smells good from the ground coffee.*

"Mom, look beside the courthouse," Jimmie said. "They've got a lean-to with Baby Jesus, Mary, and Joseph. There are other people, too."

"That's called a crèche. Those other people would be the three wise men and shepherds. I'm surprised you didn't figure that out. You know all about that from Sunday school."

"Oh, yeah. I can see that now."

"Sam, will you park in the lot behind the meat market?" Clara asked.

"That's what I planned to do. First, I'll drop you and Jimmie off in front of the Trust Building, so you won't have so far to walk. Reed can come with me while I get a couple things I need at the hardware store. We'll be back at the parking lot long before you and Jimmie return from the doctor's office."

"Probably so. It usually takes awhile to wait, especially on Saturday."

Jimmie and Clara got out and walked to the office building, then went down the hall to the elevator, which was open. They entered, and Jimmie carefully watched his mother close the door and start the lift.

I'll bet I could do that, he thought. *I wonder if we'll have any stops on the way up.*

The elevator went to the fifth floor without interruption.

As they walked down the hall, Jimmie noticed the names on the doors. *Attorney at law. That's a lawyer. I wonder what they do? There's Dr. McCracken, the dentist. That's one place I don't want to go into.*

Entering the waiting room, Clara smiled, relieved to see only four others seated there.

"I guess we won't be tied up too long," she told Jimmie.

Once they were seated, Clara looked through a stack of magazines on a nearby table. "Here's a *Life Magazine,* Jimmie. You like the pictures in that. Oh, my! Judy Garland's on the cover. You remember."

"Who?"

"Judy Garland. She's the actress we saw in *The Wizard of Oz*. She was Dorothy. Surely, you remember that."

Jimmie studied the cover. "She's a fancy lady. She don't look nothing like Dorothy."

"Anything, Jimmie, not nothing. That movie was a few years ago. Maybe she was older than she looked in the movie. Anyway, there's lots to look at in the magazine."

Halfway through the magazine, Jimmie came to the sections reporting on the war, with pictures of Navy ships and tanks. Further on were pictures of air bases in England and rows of bombers lined up ready to take off on a raid.

I think I know what those are, he thought. *Yeah. It says they're B-17s.*

"Hey, Mom, look. These are B-17s. That's the kind my cousin Ralph flew in. You can see the turret on top. That's where he was. I wonder if any of the planes in this picture are his?"

"No, Jimmie. Don't you remember? His plane was shot down, and he's been in a German prisoner of war camp for nearly a year and a half."

"Oh, yeah. That's right. It could've been an old picture."

"I guess that's possible, Jimmie, but the war's over for him, and we don't know how he's getting along. Other than being notified by the International Red Cross that he was a prisoner, all your Aunt Gayle knows is from one postcard with a few lines. Not much glory for him there. It's probably pretty rough. Think about it."

"Yeah, I guess." As he looked through the magazine, the door from the waiting room to the examining room opened, and Dr. Weiss stepped in.

"Clara, I believe it's your turn. You and Jimmie can come in now."

Jimmie didn't like being at the doctor's office, but once in the examining room, there was plenty to look at. He didn't need to be told to step up to sit on the end of the exam table. He watched the doctor sit at his desk and look through some papers.

I wonder how old he is, Jimmie thought. *Older than Dad, but he doesn't have gray hair yet. He's not as tall as Dad, but he's got a little bit of a pot gut. He seems nice, and he's never hurt me. Jerry Hickman told me how bad it hurt when the doctor set his broken arm.*

"Well, how are the Minors today?" Dr. Weiss asked.

"Everyone's in pretty good shape except Jimmie," Clara replied. "He got a cold two weeks ago, and it seems to have settled in his chest. He can't shake it."

"We'll have to see what we can do about that."

Here we go, Jimmie thought. *I wonder what'll be first. Oh, yeah. He'll use the temperature thing, then he'll ask me question, and I won't be able to answer with it in my mouth.*

"Open your shirt, Jimmie, so I can listen." He paused. "Yes, there's some congestion. Now I want to look down your throat. Stick out your tongue so I can use this swab. Say 'ah.'"

After a few minutes of looking and listening, the examination was over.

"You can button up your shirt now, Jimmie," Dr. Weiss said. "The worst is over. Clara, he has congestion in his chest, but it's not what I'd consider severe. I think it's made worse by what's going on in his throat, which is pretty inflamed. I'll need to paint it with this compound on a long cotton swab. I'll give you some, and you swab it a couple times a day. You should see some improvement in two or three days."

Jimmie had trouble not gagging when the doctor stuffed the swab down his throat, but it was over quickly.

"That's about it, Folks. Clara, did I hear you coughing in the waiting room when I came out? Do you have a cold, too?"

"No. It's probably the cigarettes."

"You should try to quit or at least cut down. I've been reading in the medical journals that they think long-term use can lead to a number of lung conditions."

"I'm not surprised, Doctor, but once you're hooked, it's tough to quit, but I'll try."

They left the building a few minutes later.

"Jimmie, I want to stop at the drugstore on the way to meet your dad and Reed."

"What will we do there?"

"I need to get some things to make some of the hard candy we usually have around Christmas—oil of wintergreen and oil of cinnamon."

"Oh, yeah. That's pretty good stuff. Will you make a lot?"

"We're low on sugar ration stamps. Frank is keeping his eye open to see if anyone has stamps they won't be using."

After a stop at the drugstore, they walked to the parking lot and saw their car with Sam and Reed beside it.

"Have you been waiting long?" Clara asked.

"No. We just got here a few minutes ago," Sam said. "How did you two make out at the doctor's office?"

"OK, I think," Clara said. "The doctor says his chest cold isn't too severe, and the main culprit is a throat infection. He gave us something for that."

"That's good. What's next?"

"I have a couple things I want to do. I still have several gifts to buy, so I'd like to spend some time at Caldwell's Department Store. I want to look in Blessings Fabric Store, too. How'd you make out at the hardware store?"

"I got most of what we needed except the copper and brass fittings to repair the hot water tank. I'll have to get a priority for those."

"What's a priority, Dad?" Reed asked.

"It's a bunch of paperwork. Certain things are in short supply, because they're needed for the military and the war effort. You have to get approval to buy them. That keeps people from buying things they don't really need and from hoarding stuff so the Army and Navy don't run short.

"Clara, the boys and I can find something to do for a while. How much time do you need for your shopping?"

"An hour should be plenty."

"That'll be fine. We'll see you back here around three-thirty."

Clara walked off in one direction, and Sam and the boys went out the parking lot to the main street.

"What will we do now, Dad?" Reed asked.

"I don't know about you two, but I'm feeling a bit hungry. How does a hotdog sound?"

"Sounds good!" the boys replied in unison.

The three went down the sidewalk easily, even though they had to share it with other pedestrians, many of whom carried bundles and bags of varying descriptions. Just ahead, a young woman dropped some of the small boxes she carried, as she tried to enter a store.

"Oh, that's Charlotte." Reed hurried ahead to where she struggled to retrieve her dropped items and hold onto others.

"Looks like you could use a little help," Reed said.

She looked up and rewarded him with a big smile. "That would be very nice, Reed. I've got more than I can handle."

"Looks like you've been doing a lot of shopping."

She smiled again. "No. This is my father's store, a lady's clothing store, and I'm helping out during the Christmas rush. I was bringing shoes over from his warehouse in the alley."

Sam and Jimmie caught up to Reed and Charlotte.

"Is this your father, Reed?" Charlotte asked, smiling at the newcomers.

"Oh, yeah. This is my dad, Sam Minor, and my little brother, Jimmie. Oh, and this is Charlotte. She's in my class at school."

"It's nice to meet you, Charlotte. I'll bet you have a last name, too." Sam had a twinkle in his eye.

"Ah, yes she does," Reed said. "It's Lang."

"Reed, you give Charlotte a hand, and Jimmie and I will go on our way. You know where to find us."

Reed helped Charlotte into the store with all her boxes.

"Thanks for your help," she said. "Your family seems nice. I think your father's a bit of a tease."

"Yeah." Reed grinned. "He can be that way. Well, see you in school."

Reed hurried outside and caught up with Sam and Jimmie in half a block.

"Is that your girlfriend?" Jimmie asked. "I think she likes you. She sure is pretty."

"I guess she is...pretty. I don't have a girlfriend. She's just a girl in my class."

Sam wisely held his tongue. *I've pulled his leg enough for one day.*

"Where will we get hotdogs, Dad?" Jimmie asked.

"We'll try the Coney Island Lunch around the corner."

They left the cold for the small eatery and were greeted by a blast of very warm air smelling of equal parts tobacco smoke and beer. They passed men sitting at stools in front of a long counter and took one of the four booths in the rear. They were sitting less than a minute when one of the men working at the stove and grill behind the counter came over to them.

"I haven't seen you in a while, Sam. These your boys?"

"Yeah, Milo. These are my sons, Reed and Jimmie. Since the school year started, I don't have much free time. You been OK?"

"Pretty good, though with the cold weather, that whack I got in the back in the Carnegie game gives me some trouble."

"Yeah. That was a tough bunch. We were lucky to win that one. We'd each like a hot dog with everything and a glass of pop. Jimmie will want orange, and Reed and I'll have Coke."

Milo left to start their orders.

"What was Carnegie about, Dad?" Reed asked.

"Milo and I were in high school together twenty years ago. We were on the football team. He was a lineman. He wasn't as big as some, but he was still a tough customer."

In a few minutes, Milo returned with their order.

"What's this stuff on top of the onions, Dad?" Jimmie asked.

"I don't know what they call it, but it sure gives a wienie a special taste. There's some meat in it and some tomato stuff, but I have no idea what the flavorings are."

They quickly devoured the food and drink, and Sam and the boys walked back outside.

"Will we go get Mom now?" Reed asked.

"I don't think it's time yet. We'll visit the five and ten on Main Street. I don't plan to buy anything, but I want to look at the men's work clothes in the basement. The sporting goods are down there, too."

Reed and Jimmie had no interest in clothing, but the sporting goods section drew them like a magnet. Reed was immediately interested in the trapping supplies.

"Are you thinking about getting more traps?" Jimmie asked.

"No. I have almost a dozen, and that's enough. A couple are pretty rusty and may not last another year, but maybe I won't trap next year. You don't get much for all that work. I was looking at the scents that are supposed to attract animals. I wonder if they work."

Jimmie shrugged. "If we had some, I could try it on my three traps."

Sam came over to the boys. "We'd better get moving and see if we can find your mother."

A short time, later, the family was together and driving out of town on the road home.

"What did you menfolk do while I was shopping?" Clara asked.

"Oh, we did a little window shopping," Sam said.

"And we had hotdogs," Jimmie added.

Clara chuckled. "I can't say that surprises me. You went to the Coney Island place?"

Sam said, "It's hard for me to pass that up."

"Any chance you got down on Chestnut Street by Montgomery Ward? I heard they were having trouble with the government, and I wondered if they were closed."

Sam said, "They were in hot water with the War Labor Board over a wage dispute. No, we didn't get down there."

"I ran into Jane Archer at the five and ten. I'll bet it's been a couple months since I last saw her."

"Have they heard anything about Clayton? Since we're back in the Philippines, I hoped they'd have some news."

"Nothing yet. My geography of the Philippines is pretty limited, but she said he was on an island called Minda something."

"That would be Mindanao. Our landings were north of there on Leyte. They seem to be working up toward Luzon, the main island."

"What's this all about?" Reed asked.

"The Archers' son, who's a few years younger than your mother and me, is an engineer who worked for a big oil company," Sam explained. "He got caught on the islands when war broke out. His family tried to find him through the Red Cross with no luck. They hope he's been able to hide somewhere. Our boys are making fast progress over there, so maybe they'll hear something soon."

As they continued toward home, the sun was low in the west, though some daylight remained.

"We should still have daylight when we get home," Sam said. "The cows will be waiting in the barnyard to get in for feed and to be milked."

"I guess the routine never changes much, does it?" Clara asked.

Twelve

After Sunday dinner, the Minor family sat around the kitchen table, savoring the memory of the repast. Clara and Sam enjoyed a second cup of coffee and cigarettes. Both boys remained at the table, though Reed pushed his chair as far back as possible to avoid the smoke.

"It seemed those scalloped potatoes could've used a little more salt, don't you think?" Clara asked no one in particular.

"Oh, they were just horrible." Reed grinned. "That's why there aren't any scraps left in the dish."

Sam chuckled. "He's got your number, all right. We should do a better job of bragging up your cooking, so you don't have to fish for compliments. If there's a better cook around, I don't know who it is."

Clara smiled, took one last drag on her cigarette, and stubbed it out. "I'd better clear things away and get the dishes done."

"Do either of you boys have any schoolwork to finish this afternoon?" Sam asked.

"Nope," they replied in union.

"We haven't gotten a Christmas tree in yet. This seems like a good time. It's not too cold today. I plan on getting two—one for us, and Lou asked me to get one for them, too."

"When are Uncle Lou and them coming to get it?"

"Don't know for sure. I told him I'd get the trees this weekend, so it wouldn't surprise me if they show up later this afternoon. 'Course, it seems he always waits till the last minute, so who knows?"

"Well," Jimmie said, "let's get started."

"Don't get in a pucker. We have all afternoon. First, you have to change out of your Sunday school clothes."

Sam and the boys were outside in the barnyard. Sam started the tractor, backed it from the shed, and pulled up near Reed and Jimmie, who waited near the wagon. A little maneuvering was required to get the wagon tongue attached to the tractor's crossbar.

"I forgot the most-important thing," Sam told Reed. "Go into the shop in the garage and get the handsaw. You boys can climb into the wagon, but be sure to sit down. The ride will be bumpy, and I don't want anyone falling out."

As Reed went for the handsaw, Jimmie walked up beside the tractor to talk to his father. "Where we gonna look for trees, Dad?"

"I thought we'd try the hollow back of the barn."

"You mean where I've been getting those pine limbs we've been selling to the teachers?"

"No. Those are too big for Christmas trees. I was thinking about the other bunch I planted on the side of the hollow near the gas well. I planted those about four or five years after the first bunch, so they should be the right size by now. I'm not supposed to harvest the whole bunch, but it's all right to thin 'em out some."

Jimmie shook his head. "Who's gonna stop you? They're our trees, aren't they?"

Sam grinned. "Yes, they are, but we got them free from the Land Conversation people, and it was understood they were to be planted in places to help stop soil erosion. They shouldn't be cut until they're mature, which is thirty or forty years."

"Is someone gonna come and check to see if they've been cut?"

"No, but it's like I made a promise to do something. You don't make promises and break them."

It was a brisk, cool day with a touch of wind, as the tractor and wagon moved down the rough trail, paralleling the small, dried-up stream that ran through the center of the small valley.

The first part of the outing took them through an area of moderate slopes that were used for pasture, though nature provided a few mature walnut trees. Farther along, the valley narrowed, and Sam geared the tractor down to climb the steeper slopes to a point where the trail gave evidence of having been excavated. A short distance along the shelf in the hillside, they reached the grove of evergreens, where Sam stopped the tractor and got down.

"Let's see what we can find," he said.

As they walked among the trees, Reed was the first to locate a prospect.

"Dad, I found a nice one. It's almost a perfect shape."

Sam walked over to look. "I don't think it'll work. It has a really good shape, but it's about two feet too tall. We'd have to cut a hole in the ceiling."

"Guess you're right."

A few minutes later, Sam said, "Here we go. I found one that'll work. It's the right height, and the shape is good."

"It doesn't look very tall to me," Jimmie said.

"Remember, we'll be using a stand, and we have to allow room at the top for the star."

"OK." He nodded.

Reed walked around behind the tree and studied it. "A couple rows up, there's another one about this size, and it looks pretty good. Come take a look."

They walked to the next one.

Sam rubbed his chin and nodded. "Yes. This will do all right."

"It looks pretty scrubby on this side," Jimmie said.

"I know, but we can put our tree in the parlor corner. The bad side can be out of sight, and it'll look fine. The first one we saw can be for Lou's family. They don't always put their tree in the same place, and a bad area might show."

It took only a few minutes to cut down the two trees and load them into the wagon. On the way back to the house, Reed stood on the crossbar behind the tractor, holding onto the driver's seat. That left Jimmie sitting in the wagon between the two trees.

That pine really smells good, Jimmie thought. *This is the first real sign that Christmas is coming. I wonder when we'll put up the tree and start to decorate it. It probably won't be for a couple days, so it won't dry out too soon. What will I get for Christmas? Probably clothes and toys. Mom asked a couple days ago if I ever wanted to try ice skating. Maybe I'll get skates. That would be nice. I hope she has an idea what I can get for Reed.*

Jimmie's reverie quickly ended, as they reached the barnyard, and Sam drove the wagon beyond the garage to shorten the distance they'd have to carry the trees to the house. Seeing a car parked in the lane, they recognized it as belonging to Sam's brother, Lou.

Hurrying inside, they were greeted by a blast of warm air and the sweet, aromatic smell of Clara's candy making. They found Clara and Lou sitting at the kitchen table, drinking coffee and smoking, and exchanged greetings.

"We got you a really nice Christmas tree, Uncle Lou," Jimmie said.

"I was counting on it, Jimmie. I'm sure it'll look great once it's decorated."

"How's the family, Lou?" Sam asked.

"I was just telling Clara that Bonnie's fine, and the kids are in good shape. Joey's coming off a cold he's had for a few days, but it didn't amount to much. He was hoping for a few days off from school, but Bonnie sent him anyway, and it all worked out. Before I forget, we're expecting you folks to come to our place for Christmas night."

"That'll be really nice," Clara said. "It'll be fun to visit. I'm looking forward to seeing how Bonnie decorated your place for the holiday."

Lou laughed. "That might depend on whether or not those wild Indians of ours have destroyed everything by the time you get there. I'll need help getting rid of all the ham and turkey she plans to have. Otherwise, that's all I'll get for two weeks."

"Speaking of eating, why not stay for supper? I'll be making that soon."

"No thanks, Clara. I appreciate the offer, but I need to get back. Bonnie's expecting me, and I have paperwork to do this evening."

A few minutes later, Sam and Lou retrieved the pine tree from the wagon and struggled to get it into the car trunk.

"It'll hang out a good bit," Sam said, "but we can use binder twine to tie down the lid. That should hold."

"I believe that'll do it. By the way, have you heard the news?"

"No. Did you hear something?"

"I'm not sure. I had the car radio on while I drove here. The reception wasn't very good with all the static I get, but I thought a heard something about a German offensive."

"That's news to me. I thought things quieted down over there until the weather was better. We sure don't need things to get any more heated. I read a little piece in the paper the other day that said our total casualties in all the war theaters has gone over 550,000 since the damn thing started. That's over half a million lives wasted. Sometimes, it seems people can't get enough of killing each other. They chased the Krauts out of Greece, and now they've got a civil war, with the commies trying to take over."

Sam paused. "I'll have to make a point to listen to the six-o'clock news and see what's up. Anyway, I hope you have a good Christmas. Weather permitting, we'll see you that evening."

Sam watched his brother back the car out of the lane and head toward town. *The roads are good,* he thought, *and they aren't calling for snow, so I guess he'll get home OK. It's almost dark now. I'd better get to the barn and start work. I'd like to hear the news at six, though there usually isn't much to report on Sunday night. Sometimes it's nothing.*

Later, Sam was in the barn, milking the next-to-last cows. *This place that used to be the horse stable worked pretty well for the milking area. I hated spending the money on metal stanchions from Sears and all the concrete the boys and I laid out, but I don't know how many times the inspector from the milk company stopped by to look it over. He said he saw how careful I tried to be to keep things clean, but the company didn't like the old dirt floors. They wanted me to modernize.*

He smiled at the memory. *Urging? I wasn't born yesterday, and I could read between the lines. The choices were to improve the operation, or they wouldn't buy my milk anymore. That's not much of a choice. In the summer when I don't have any teaching checks coming in, the milk money is almost our only source of cash.*

He checked his watch. *It's almost six. I won't finish in time to hear the news in the house. Let's see how this old radio tunes in today.*

He walked to the radio and turned it on, waiting for it to warm up. Finally, he heard music. He turned the other knob and was rewarded by a different kind of music. It stopped, and an announcer came on.

"Ladies and Gentlemen, we interrupt our usual Sunday evening music program to bring you an important news story. Details are limited and incomplete, but it's clear from reports filed by individual war correspondents, as well as the Associated Press, that the Germans have initiated a major offensive in the area of the Ardennes and through Belgium.

"What was originally thought to be a series of minor scouting probes has been confirmed by Allied headquarters as a major offensive along an eighteen-mile front involving as many as several hundred German tanks and armored vehicles and thousands of crack infantry units. The Luftwaffe put at least 1,000 single-engine fighters and bombers into the air to support the offensive.

"Military experts say this is Germany greatest demonstration of offensive aerial strength since the Battle of Britain in 1940. Early reports indicate there have been heavy casualties on both sides. As additional reports are received, this station will interrupt its regular programming to keep our listeners informed."

As the music resumed, Sam shook his head. *They must have an idiot picking their tunes. I can't think of anything more inappropriate than* Jingle Bells *after hearing that. I'd better finish the milking and get inside. Clara will want to know about this.*

When the family gathered at the kitchen table, all reflected on the news.

"Did they say where this is happening?" Reed asked. "Is it in France?"

"I'm a little fuzzy on the geography," Sam said, "but I think it's north of there, somewhere in Belgium. They said the attack came through the Ardennes, and that's rugged, hilly area."

"If memory serves me correctly," Clara said, "isn't that the same area through which the Germans launched their attack on France back in 1940?"

"I believe you're right. The French thought they were safe behind their fortifications along the German border. The Krauts went up and around them. Somebody wasn't thinking very good."

"Is any of this happening where Rex is?" Reed asked.

"He's somewhere over there, but we don't know exactly when," Clara replied. "Oh, my. That's something else for poor Gayle to worry about."

Sam shook his head. "Seems like a hell of a way to usher in the Christmas season."

"Anyway," Clara said, "Bob Hope will be on later tonight. He's usually pretty funny, so maybe that'll give us a lift."

"Maybe, but since the war started, he's been taking USO shows to the military camps here in this country and overseas during the Christmas season. It could be he might not be on tonight. We'll have to wait and see."

Thirteen

Clara put bacon in the skillet to fry for breakfast and sat at the kitchen table with her first cup of coffee and a cigarette when Sam came in from outside with a bucket of milk in each hand.

"Lord, it's cold out there!" he said.

"I can believe it by seeing your red cheeks. You should be ready for breakfast now. How do you want your eggs this morning?"

"Fried, I guess. Hmmm. That bacon smells good. Tell you what, though. Hold up on the eggs. I have to strain this milk into the cans, and I'll shave for work before I eat. I might enjoy eating more after I've thawed out a bit."

Clara nodded.

Sometime later, Sam finished his breakfast, and they both drank coffee. Clara lit a cigarette.

"I might as well have a smoke, too," Sam said. "I never smoke when I'm around the barn. At work, I don't have much chance except when I have a free period or lunch in the teacher's room."

"I'm afraid I'd have a tough time of it if I was still teaching. I smoke a lot more than before we married, when only single women could teach. I wonder why they had that rule?"

"I never heard what was behind that. I guess someone thought married women should be at home, being housewives."

"It's a good thing someone came to his senses and did away with that. You can bet lots of women working in the defense plants are married."

"I'm sure that's the case. It's getting late. I need to get changed and get going. You have any special plans today?"

"Yes, I do. The Missionary Society meeting is today at Mildred Bristor's. After the boys leave, I plan to bake a ham loaf for the potluck lunch. This being a Christmastime meeting, everyone is supposed to bring a Pollyanna, and we're having a gift exchange."

"What are you taking?"

"A nice head scarf I got the other week when we were in town. Nobody was supposed to spend more than a dollar."

"You'll be lucky to come home with a jar of green beans. Some of those folks don't have two nickels to rub together."

"They do what they can. Did you have the radio on while you were milking? Is there any more war news?"

"Yes, I had it on. There's nothing more than what they said last night. Will Frank take you and Ester to the meeting?"

"That's the plan."

The meeting lasted longer than usual, but Clara was the first of the family to return home in midafternoon. Within the next hour and a half, the other family members arrived. Jimmie took his sled to get more pine boughs. Reed brought the dairy cattle to the milk stable and pitched hay to the beef cattle by the time Sam was home. He sat in the kitchen to lace up his boots before going out to the barn.

"How'd the meeting go?"

"OK, I guess," Clara replied. "It was a little longer than usual."

"Oh? Why was that?"

"The turnout was bigger than usual, so that made the lunch longer. Then the gift exchange took time."

"What did you get, a jar of green beans?

Clara smiled. "A little better than that. It was a jar of spiced pears from Jane Hartzell. That's something I don't put up, and they'll be a nice side dish at Christmas."

"At least you didn't get skunked like some times."

"Oh, yes. I almost forgot. We had a lengthy discussion during the business meeting."

"What was that about?"

"Whether to raise the price of the quilts we make. Along with the church suppers we have, the sale of quilts is an important source of funds we give to national missions. Some of us think we ought to raise the price from twelve to fifteen dollars."

"A price increase doesn't sound unreasonable. Other things are going up. If you put any value to your time, you aren't making much."

"How do you figure that?"

"When you add the quilting frames set up here in the parlor, it was about six weeks. You probably had four women here, maybe three or four nights a week, for a couple hours. At twelve dollars a quilt, your labor alone probably came to ten or twelve cents an hour. Minimum wage is forty cents, though I hear the Democrats want to raise it to sixty cents. You aren't making much at twelve dollars. If you were a business, you'd go broke pretty quick."

"I should've had those numbers with me. I was in favor of the increase. As it turned out, it was put off until next month."

"So much for that. Time for me to get out to the barn and get the milking done."

A little while later, Sam walked into the cow stable and had to push cats away with his boot.

"You bunch of beggars are out of luck tonight. I'm doing the milking, not the boys."

He smiled at the thought of Reed and Jimmie squirting milk at the cats, trying to hit their open mouths. *I might as well turn on the radio and see if there's any news,* he thought.

"Mairzy doats and dozy doats and liddle lamzy divey...."

Oh, my God. That's the dumbest song I ever heard. I wonder what crazy person came up with that? Let's see if I can find some news.

"Ladies and Gentlemen, we have an update on the fighting associated with the German offensive in the Ardennes area of Belgium and Luxemburg, which began yesterday. A few hours ago, the Associated Press reported that the German armored forces penetrated at least eighteen miles into areas previously occupied by Allied forces. Some military strategists speculated that the offensive has a two-fold objective.

"In the first instance, they say the German hope to divide the British and Canadian forces in the north from the American forces, thus hampering coordination of Allied tactical efforts. It is also believed that the main objective of the thrust is the port of Antwerp. The port facilities there have become the principle location for supplying fuel, munitions, and other materials required by the armed forces. The artificial docking facilities called Mulberries used for this purpose in the immediate aftermath of D-Day were damaged beyond repair by storms. The capture of Antwerp would be a serious blow to the supply efforts of the Allies.

"In other news, the fighting in the Pacific is much more positive. Efforts by a Japanese convoy to reinforce and resupply their troops in the Philippines were thwarted when U.S. Naval forces sank twenty-eight enemy ships and damaged sixty-six others.

"In other action, B-29 Superfortresses caused extensive damage to the Mitsubishi aircraft works in a raid at Nagoya on the Japanese mainland.

"In other news, word has been received that a plane carrying band leader Glenn Miller from England to an undisclosed location in Allied-occupied areas in France has been reported missing. Search planes crisscrossing a wide area of the English Channel have been unsuccessful in their efforts to locate wreckage or survivors."

That doesn't sound very good in Europe, Sam thought. *I hope they have some reserves they can use to stem the tide, and I hope it isn't worse than what's been reported. Doesn't sound good about Glenn Miller, either.*

Fourteen

"Could I have mashed potatoes, please, Mom?" Jimmie asked.

"Sure. There's plenty. How about you, Sam and Reed? Pass them down, Jimmie."

The family sat at the kitchen table, eating their evening meal. The sun dipped below the horizon an hour earlier, so it was pitch dark outside.

"I'll be very glad when the days start getting longer in a few weeks," Sam said. "It's depressing to get up when it's dark and not have daily chores finished before dark."

Clara nodded. "Yes, and your work isn't finished. You probably have quizzes to correct or other work to prepare for tomorrow."

"I almost forgot to tell you. They pulled the winning tickets for the Christmas raffle at the teachers' meeting after school, and I won the top prize."

"What'd you get, Dad?" Reed asked. "A new pencil for marking down grades?"

"Very funny. It's a lot better than that. I got a twenty-pound Christmas turkey."

"What'll we do with it?" Clara asked. "We already ordered our turkey from Longdon's Market and gave them our ration tickets."

"This kind of stuff is off the books as far as ration tickets are concerned. It's being donated by the brother of Sally Summers, the music teacher. He has a small farm over by Amity and raises a few turkeys. I can pick it up on the way home on the Thursday before Christmas."

Clara frowned and shook her head. "That's all well and good, but it still doesn't answer the question of what we'll do with it. We can't eat two turkeys."

"That's true, and there isn't enough room in the food locker for a whole bird, but maybe, if we cut it into pieces we can get it in."

"That seems possible."

"Maybe we ought to give it to someone, it bein' Christmas and all," Reed said.

"Yeah," Jimmie said. "That's a great idea. We were all talking about what we hoped we'd get for Christmas at Sunday school, and Mrs. Hackney told us not to forget that it's better to give than to receive."

Clara and Sam exchanged smiles.

"It's good someone around here remembers what Christmas is all about," Sam said. "Who should we give it to?"

"I can think of one possibility," Clara said. "At the Mission-ary Society meeting last week, they said the Craft family was having a tough time."

"I expect that's right. Mahlon was banged up pretty bad with an accident at the sawmill where he works. He's probably been out of work for the better part of a month. I imagine they're running short on just about everything."

"Eddie's in my class," Jimmie said. "When it's not too cold, we eat our lunch at our fort in the woods. All he ever has in his lunch bucket is a sandwich of homemade bread with nothin' between the slices except yellow mustard. He also brings an orange. He says they get the oranges from relief. What's relief?"

"That's from the government to help folks who are short on money," Sam explained.

"OK. I guess they'd have oranges and bread to eat with their turkey."

Clara smiled. "It might be nice if we could come up with some other things to go with it. Maybe we can make up a box of things for their Christmas dinner. Wouldn't that be nice?"

"Sounds good to me. What else can we put in?"

"Let's see. For starters, I'm sure we have enough potatoes in the cellar to spare a few. I've got more jars of green beans and applesauce put up than we can use before next summer. That's a start. I've also got a bunch of stale bread and crusts I've been saving to make dressing. It's more than we need. You could cut those up for me, and we'll send along a bag."

"I just thought of something," Sam said. "Those molasses cookies you made before Thanksgiving and put into those cookie tins should be softened and ready by now. We could add some of those."

"Good idea. We've got a little more than a week. Everyone should think of what else we can come up with."

"I'm starting to wonder something," Reed said slowly.

"What's that, Son?" Sam asked.

"It was my idea in the first place, but do you think they might not like it if we're giving them all this, like we're better than them or lordin' it over them somehow?"

Sam rubbed his chin and thought for a moment. "I don't think so, Reed. Mahlon's always struck me as a man who's got his head on right. I'm pretty sure they'll just be grateful. When we take the stuff over, we'll make it a point to say we had extra and not hang around like we wanted to be thanked."

He thought a little longer, then added, "One other thing— this is nobody's business except us and the Craft family. I want you boys to keep this to yourself and not tell your friends. If it gets around, it'll start to look like we're trying to get patted on the back. That's not the idea. We're doing this, because it's the right thing to do."

The boys nodded.

"Look at the time," Sam said. "We've been sitting here jawing, and the first thing you know, I'll miss the evening news. I expect they have a new report on that German attack."

He stood and left the kitchen.

"Why is Dad so interested in the war news?" Jimmie asked.

"It's more than just curiosity," Clara replied. "Your father's an intelligent man and a good citizen. He thinks, and rightly so, that it's important to be informed about what's happening in the world, so good decisions can be made about things that affect us. He's well thought of in the community, and lots of people ask his opinion on all sorts of matters. That's why he agreed to serve on the school board last year after several people asked him."

Fifteen

"Clara, what time does the church program start?"

"Seven-thirty, Sam."

"All right. That'll work. I'll have time to listen to the news and shave before we have to start out."

"Just keep in mind I need to get there a few minutes early. I made cookies to put in with the other stuff for a treat for the little kids."

"What will they have for them?"

"I think they have candy, and someone's making popcorn balls. A couple of other women are making cookies, and the kids will all get an orange."

"Did they get the oranges from Frank?"

Clara grinned. "Yes, but he wasn't too happy about it. He doesn't ordinarily buy much fruit of any kind from them in town, and they wouldn't give him a wholesale price, so he won't make anything."

"What are oranges going for?"

"The last I saw when we were in town, they were forty-nine cents a dozen."

"That's not such a big loss for him. I'd better stop jawing and get out to the barn and get started." He left the kitchen.

As he walked out to the barn, Sam thought about the chores. *Milking shouldn't take too long, with four of the seven dairy cows dried up. The way it's going, we'll be lucky to have one can of milk to sell next week. Good thing we don't have to rely on milk money as our only source of cash, like we did before I was lucky and got that teaching job in '39. That was a godsend.*

Sometime later, after returning from the barn and eating dinner, Sam settled into his easy chair and turned on the radio on the adjacent table. As usual, it took several seconds for the tubes to warm up.

His ears were assaulted by static. *Damn! When I had this on this afternoon, the station was clear as a bell. I'll have to tune it in, as usual.*

Adjusting the dial, he eventually found clarity of sound that consisted of a Christmas carol. Looking at the clock, he nodded. It was five minutes before six, so he had to be patient.

The evening broadcast began with war news.

"The German offensive through the Ardennes area of Belgium continues. Allied headquarters today confirmed that the enemy actions that began the previous Sunday were indeed a major initiative. Spokesmen for the Allies admitted that in some places enemy-armored Panzer units advanced as far as thirty-five miles into areas previously held by units of the U.S. Army. There is some indication that the offensive has been blunted or at least slowed in the south. American forces, including the 101st Airborne, have stubbornly resisted German advances in the key area of the Belgium town of Bastogne, an important junction of several roads.

"In the Pacific, Japanese attempts to supply and reinforce their units in the Philippines have been thwarted with the loss of numerous ships and planes. Nevertheless, they maintain a stiff resistance to the advance of our forces. Meanwhile, B-29s continue to hammer military and manufacturing targets on the Japanese homeland.

"Finally, in military matters, President Roosevelt today signed papers awarding General Eisenhower a fifth star and promotion to the rank of General of the Army."

Sam turned off the radio, as Clara came into the living room.

"What's the news tonight?" she asked.

"It sounds like we're in a bit of a pickle in Belgium. As near as I can tell, our boys haven't been able to get this latest German attack stopped and reversed. It's hard to say. Sometimes, I think we don't get the whole story. It seems that when things don't go well, they get vague in their descriptions. If it's going pretty good, they make it sound like a major victory."

Clara nodded.

"I'd better wash off that cow smell and shave. I suppose you want to leave for church around seven?"

"That sounds about right."

A short time later, Reed and Jimmie dressed for the service and waited in the living room.

"Reed," Sam called from the bathroom, "would you do something for me? I'm finishing up shaving and have to get dressed. Would you get a bucket of water and put it in the car radiator?"

"Sure. When do you figure we'll get that leak fixed?"

"Probably Saturday morning. I've got the solder and everything to do the job. There just isn't time in the morning or after I'm home from school. In the meantime, we have to keep draining it overnight to keep it from freezing. Antifreeze is too expensive to put it in and have it leak out every day."

"Need any help, Reed?" Jimmie asked.

"No, thanks. It's a one-man job. You might as well stay here and keep warm. Dad, should I start the car so it can warm up by the time we're ready to go?"

"Yeah. That's a good idea."

Only a few cars parked near the church when they arrived. Sam found a parking spot close to the front, where the accumulated snow was packed down.

Once inside the vestibule, Clara walked into the young peoples' Sunday school area, where she and several other women began assembling the Christmas treats to be given to the youngsters. Sam and the boys hung up their coats and went into the church sanctuary. Sam and Jimmie went to the area where the family usually sat, while Reed joined the teenagers in the rear pews.

Jimmie noticed curtains obscuring the raised area at the front of the church where the altar from which the preacher usually spoke and the piano and choir sections were located.

"Looks like there'll be a performance, Dad," Jimmie said.

"Usually is. Don't you remember from last year?"

"I forgot."

Jimmie twisted in his seat to watch members come into the sanctuary and take their seats. *I wonder why they always sit in the same places?* he thought.

To his surprise, Old Mr. Shriever didn't take his usual place with his wife but went to sit in the front row.

I guess he'll start the program, and Reverend French can't make it tonight. Hmmm. He's one of the elders, whatever that means.

Jimmie was so intent on studying the front of the church that he failed to see Clara come in from the rear until she sat beside Sam.

"Looks like we'll have a big turnout," Clara said softly.

"Yeah. It isn't bitter cold, and the roads are pretty good, so there's no excuse to stay home."

A few minutes later, after the latecomers entered, Elder Shriever stood, checked his pocket watch for the time, walked to the center of the altar area, and cleared his throat. All conversation ceased. As those assembled looked toward him expectantly, he nodded and smiled.

"Well, Folks, I'm afraid you have a poor substitute this night. Reverend French asked me to fill in. He's down with a cold. It's nothing serious, but he wants to try to get over it by Sunday. Christmas Eve falls on Sunday only every few years, so he wants to be part of that.

"We're here tonight for the Christmas program. It'll be a pleasant experience, I'm sure, but we must remember that this is the season that we celebrate God's greatest gift to mankind—the birth of Jesus. Keeping that in mind, let's begin with a prayer.

"Our Father in Heaven, we give thanks for the opportunity to share in this evening's fellowship. We look forward to the activities that will strengthen our understanding of what the Christmas season is about. We thank You for the talents You have given to all those who will participate in the program.

"Lord, please be with our servicemen stationed around the world, most especially those fellows who are having a tough time of it with the Germans. In Christ's name, amen.

"To begin this evening's program, we'll have scripture readings by two of our senior high Sunday school members. First, Cora Grim will read from the second chapter of the gospel of Saint Luke. That will be followed by a portion of the second chapter of the gospel of Saint Matthew, read by Reed Minor."

A teenage girl walked briskly to the front of the church, turned, and began reading. "And it came to pass in those days that there went out a decree from Caesar Augustus...."

She read the balance of the twenty verses that described the birth of the Christ child in the stable in Bethlehem and the appearance of the angels to nearby shepherds, who went to see Mary, Joseph, and baby Jesus.

Cora retreated to the rear of the church, and Reed walked to the front to begin his reading.

"Now when Jesus was born in Bethlehem in the days of Herod the king, behold there came wise men from the east to Jerusalem." He read the twelve verses describing the wise men following the star to Bethlehem, how they found and worshipped Mary and the baby and gave gifts, and how they left the Holy Land without telling Herod the location of Jesus.

Reed returned to his seat, and Elder Shriever stood to continue the program. With a smile, he said, "The next thing on the evening's activities is music. I know you'll be pleased to find out I won't lead the singing."

A few chuckles broke out.

"Fortunately, our choir director, Marion, is here this evening to handle that. Though you can't see her, Mildred is at her usual place at the piano behind the curtains. Marion, if you would, please."

"Thank you, Elder. We have two songs to set the mood for the sketch. It's not long enough to call a play. The first is *Oh, Little Town of Bethlehem*, number 127 in the hymnal.

"When you're ready, Mildred."

The piano began playing the introductory bars to the song. Marion gestured to the congregation, and they began singing. That song was followed by *Hark the Herald Angels Sing*. At the conclusion of the second song, Marion disappeared behind the sheet. They heard shuffling feet and the sound of moving furniture, then a few seconds of silence. When the piano began playing *Away in the Manger*, the curtains were drawn back.

The audience saw the traditional view of a stable with a man and woman in period clothing representing Joseph and Mary. A boxlike structure near the woman was the manger. Someone painted a cardboard backdrop to represent the interior of a stable with animals in the stalls.

The piano played briefly, and the actors remained motionless. When the music ended, they engaged in a brief dialogue about the hardship of their trip from Nazareth and how fortunate they were to find the shelter where their baby was born.

Four shepherds entered, knelt by the manger, and told Mary and Joseph how they were visited by angels who told them of the birth of the Christ child.

After the shepherds left the stable, another group came in to represent the three wise men. They presented gifts to the baby and knelt in a worshipful manner. Before they left the stable, they warned Mary and Joseph that King Herod meant to harm the Child.

As Mary and Joseph bowed their heads in prayer, the curtain closed. The audience applauded briefly. The choir director returned from behind the curtain and announced the final song would be *Silent Night.*

When the last notes of the song ended, no one moved to leave, because the evening's activities weren't finished. Elder Shriever stood and faced the group.

"Now we've been reminded what Christmas is really about, it's time for the fun part of the evening. As usual, we have a Christmas treat for the youngsters that our church ladies put together. Harriet, will you and Juanita bring those boxes full of treat bags over here and get ready to hand them out? You young folks come up, form a line, and we'll get started."

The quiet decorum of the evening broke down a bit, as young people left the pews and walked to the front. Children and adults began talking. A few of the older people without children stood and moved out of the sanctuary. In a few minutes, the distribution of treats was completed, and the balance of the congregation went outside into the cold night.

The silence in the car, as the Minor family drove home, was finally broken by Reed.

"Well, Squirt, what did you get in the bag? The usual stuff?"

Jimmie had already inspected the bag's contents, but he checked again before saying, "It's a pretty good haul. There's an orange, a popcorn ball, some candy, and several cookies."

"I'd say you were pretty fortunate," Sam said. "I wouldn't be surprised if tonight's treat is all the Christmas some of the kids get. At least a couple of the families I saw there are on relief, so they don't have much.

"Since the war started, a few of the folks around here were lucky and got defense work. They're doing OK. My cousin Alton, who lived near Washington, moved somewhere in Beaver County to work at a defense plant. I think he's making airplane propellers. Some others got work in the Pittsburgh area, but there's many other good folks from around here who are still trying to scratch out some kind of living on their farms. That's a pretty tough way to make a go of it."

Sixteen

The sun was low in the afternoon sky when Sam pulled into the lane and stopped the car near the wagon shed. He started to open the rear side door to get something out, then he paused, shook his head, closed the door, and went into the house. Without removing his outer clothing, he walked into the kitchen.

"Hi, Dad," Jimmie said.

"Hi, Son. Where's your mom?"

"I'm right here in the junk room," Clara said, stepping into the kitchen. You're a few minutes later than usual."

"I had to pick up that turkey. It's in the car, and I thought this would be a good time to take it up to the Crafts. Do we have the other stuff ready?"

"Pretty much. It'll take only a few seconds to get it into a box. Jimmie, why don't you get your coat and cap, and you can go along and help your dad?"

"Has Reed come home from school yet?" Sam asked.

"Yes," Clara said. "He got out early. He already got the cows in and started milking."

"That's a big help. Jimmie, would you look in the junk room? One of my wreaths is on the wall behind the separator. We might just as well take that along. Maybe they could use it as a decoration for their door."

In a few minutes, Sam and Jimmie were walking to the car. Sam carried a large box of food, and Jimmie had the wreath. They set the items in the back seat beside the turkey and were soon on their way.

"Do you know where the Crafts live, Dad?"

"I never visited them, but they're in the old Pratt place."

"How do we get there?"

"Just up the way like we're going to church, then we turn off on that red-dog road past Eppley's barn."

Jimmie paused and thought about that. "Why are those old back roads called red dog?"

Sam smiled. "It's from the stones they spread on them so we don't have to drive in mud. They're kind of red."

"Yeah. They're really strange. Most of the stones I see are brown."

"The red dog comes from the coal mines near the river. It's waste material from the mines, along with some low-grade coal they can't sell. It's in big piles, and they sometimes catch fire and smolder a long time. That's what makes it red. The township gets it for free. It's better than nothing to stop the mud."

Sam slowed the car. "Here's where we turn off. It's a little over a mile to where we're going."

They entered the secondary road, where their travel was much slower. The red-dog surface wasn't conducive to fast travel, but it was also very narrow. In many places they saw ditches on one or both sides.

"What will we do if we meet an oncoming car?" Jimmie asked.

Sam smiled. "Someone would have to back up until we found a place where he could pull off and let the other fellow past, but it isn't likely. There aren't more than three or four houses down this road."

There wasn't much to see. Most of the areas along the road were covered with trees and brush.

"There don't seem to be any pastures or fields to plant corn and wheat up here, Dad. Why?"

"It's pretty hilly and not very good for grain. The soil's too thin. The farms up here never amounted to much. Most people up this way are lucky to have gardens and grow a few things, but they can't make a living off the land. They have to work for someone else to make ends meet."

"I guess since Mr. Craft was hurt, they've had it kind of rough."

"That's about the size of it, Jimmie. Our destination is around the next curve in the road."

Sam slowed the car and parked in front of the house beside another car that had lots of rust along the sides and fenders. He and Jimmie looked around without speaking for a few seconds.

"I haven't come up this way in a few years," Sam said. "It never was a showplace, but I can't believe how rundown it's become."

Jimmie shook his head. He saw traces of what looked like yellow paint, but most of the structure looked gray and weathered. The porch roof was pulling away from the side of the house, caused by the supports leaning outward. Half the rain gutter hung loose from the roof edge. One of the second-story windows was covered with boards. The roof was patched in several places, and smoke came from a chimney that was missing a couple of top bricks. A glance out back revealed three outbuildings and a small barn in equally bad shape.

"Well, we're here," Sam said. "Might as well get this over with. Mind your manners."

They walked to the front porch with boxes of food. A large brown dog lying in front of the door got up and moved a few feet away.

Sam chuckled. "He may not be friendly, but at least he isn't mean." He knocked.

They heard shuffling feet and muted conversation. A middle-aged woman opened the door halfway.

"Yes?"

"Afternoon, Mrs. Craft. You may not remember me, but I'm Sam Minor. I believe I've seen you a few times down at the store with Mahlon."

"Oh, yes. That's so. This must be Jimmie. Our boy, Eddie, talks about him a lot."

"Who is it, Lena?" a voice called from inside.

"It's Mr. Minor and Jimmie."

"Well, ask them in, for pity's sake. It's gotta be cold out there on the porch."

Inside the living room, the furnishings and housekeeping were similar to the impression Sam and Jimmie gained from outside. A badly worn sofa, partially covered by a torn quilt, dominated the far side of the room. Other seating consisted of three battered wooden chairs. A large table to one side was piled high with papers, a basket of clothing, and several dirty dishes. The main feature of the room was a large, pot-bellied stove. Chopped and split wood in a wooden fruit crate sat to one side.

They heard a scuffling sound, and Mahlon Craft moved through a curtain and into the living room using a makeshift crutch. He gritted his teeth in pain, but he managed a smile for the visitors.

"Sam, it's good of you to stop by. We don't get many visitors up this way. What brings you by? What in the world do you and Jimmie have in those boxes?"

"Maybe some things you folks can use to add to your Christmas dinner." He set down the box on the table and nodded for Jimmie to do the same.

"We ended up with more than we could use," Sam explained. "We'd already ordered a turkey from Longdons, and I won one at the raffle the teachers had in a school. We couldn't handle both, so we thought maybe you could take one off our hands. Clara put in few other things. I'm not sure what.

"Oh. I almost forgot. Most years, I make wreaths for decorating and the cemetery. It turned out I had one more than I needed, so you're welcome to that."

"Sam, I don't know how to thank you. Things have been kinda tough around here. I don't know if we'd have had much of a big feed for Christmas if'n it weren't for this."

"You folks are welcome. How soon will you get back to work?"

"Hard to say. This bum leg's coming along, but it's got a ways to go."

"I'm sure you want to get back to work as soon as possible, but you don't want to rush it. Get back too soon and aggravate it, you might end up off work even longer. They still busy at the sawmill?"

"Yeah. At least, we were back when I was hurt. It's not like it was a year and a half ago when the government was pushing hard for every board foot. I dunno...maybe for barracks and other stuff. The boss is trying to line up other wood lots. He says when this is over, and the fellas come home, there'll be new families and a big demand for homes."

"Makes sense to me."

During a pause, Jimmie asked, "Where's Eddie?"

"He and his brothers are out chasing cows. The line fence between us and Sibert's isn't kept up very good, and our cows went visitin'. They don't amount to much, but there's two that haven't gone dry yet, so we get a little milk."

"Speakin' of milkin'," Sam said, "Jimmie and I'd better be on our way. We need to get home to help Reed finish that chore."

Lena, who'd been silent so far, said, "Hold on a minute before you leave. I have something for you folks."

She left the way Mahlon walked in. They heard a door open and close, then she returned.

"I know Clara doesn't bake bread, and I was busy at that the whole forenoon. I want you folks to have these two fresh loaves. You can't beat the taste of home-baked."

"That's a fact, Lena. Thanks. I know we'll enjoy it."

Sam and Jimmie left and drove back in the car. Both were silent for a while.

"I think we did a good thing, Dad," Jimmie said. "It kinda makes me feel good."

"I agree. I'm afraid those folks don't have much even in the best of times. With Mahlon being hurt and no money coming in, it has to be tough."

"It was nice of Missus Craft to give us that bread. I bet it tastes really good."

"I'm sure it does. Jimmie, a loaf of bread costs nine cents at the store. That might not seem like much, but I'd be surprised if you could find as much as one thin dime in that household. It was a very nice gesture on her part."

Sam glanced at his wristwatch without success. "It's dark enough that I can't see the time, but it must be after five. We stayed longer at the Crafts than I planned. We need to get home. If Reed isn't finished milking, we should give him a hand. Mom's planning for us to decorate the Christmas tree tonight."

Sam pushed his chair back from the table. "I'll take a few minutes to try to catch the news before we start on the tree. I haven't heard anything all day, and I'm anxious to know what's going on with that German attack."

Ignoring Clara's frown, he went into the living room. Those who remained in the kitchen heard static from the radio, as Sam tried to tune into his preferred station. After several seconds, they faintly heard the broadcast.

Sam leaned closer to the radio, listening carefully.

"Ladies and Gentlemen, we have mixed news tonight regarding the German offensive in the Ardennes. The Associated Press reports that the German forces have made little or no advance to the west in the last twenty-four to thirty-six hours. However, Panzer units have been tightening the noose around the strategic town of Bastogne. American forces, including the crack 101st Airborne, are waging a stiff defense in the face of resupply efforts hampered by poor flying conditions. Elements of General Patton's Third army are fighting from the south to relieve their beleaguered comrades. The extent of their progress hasn't been revealed. In the Pacific, our troops continue to make steady progress in Luzon and are pushing the Japanese back on all fronts."

That sounds somewhat better, Sam thought. *Still, those fellows must be having a tough time. Yesterday, someone said they were having the coldest winter in memory in Europe. I sure can't do anything about that. I guess I'd better get back and work on that tree.*

In the kitchen, Clara heard the radio stop and said, "Jimmie, why don't you go into the parlor and see if you can help your dad. Maybe you can untangle the tree lights. They're usually a mess. Reed's drying dishes for me, so we'll be in there soon to help."

When Jimmie entered the parlor, he was greeted by the pleasant odor of pine needles. His dad brought in the tree the previous day so the limbs would open up. The rest of the room was in serious disorder. A variety of boxes, some opened, were scattered on the floor. Others sat on the sofa, with a few more on the piano.

"Mom said I should come in to help," Jimmie told Sam.

"Good idea. I can use the help. That large box on the sofa has the tree lights. Take them out very carefully and get them untangled on the floor. Don't bang the bulbs together, because you might damage them. We'll have to test them to see if they all work. I was able to get only a few replacements. We'll have to be real careful. While you do that, I want to see if the ornaments survived another year."

Jimmie soon had all three strands of colored lights laid out on the floor. When he tested them by plugging them into an extension cord from the wall socket, he saw two of the three strands didn't light.

"We've got problems with two of them, Dad," he said.

"All right. The new bulbs are in this bag. You'll have to carefully unscrew each bulb and put in one of the good ones. Keep doing that until the strand lights up. Then you'll know you found the bad one."

Jimmie succeeded with the first strand almost immediately. The second required more time, since it had two defective bulbs.

"OK, Dad. We're all set."

"Good. Unplug the extension cord and let them cool off. I don't want to put them on the tree while they're still warm. That's more apt to break the filament."

Clara and Reed entered the parlor.

"We've got everything cleaned up in the kitchen," Clara said. "Looks like we're about ready to start decorating the tree."

Sam said, "Jimmie has the lights all squared away, and I'm ready to start opening boxes of ornaments. We'll have to be very careful with them. They're fragile and easy to break."

"Couldn't we get new ones if some were broken?" Jimmie asked.

"Not easily, if at all. Most of these we've had for many years. They're molded from very thin glass. I believe they came from Germany or Austria. With the war on, there haven't been any available for several years. I wonder when the war's over if they'll start making them again."

They arranged the lights on the tree, then the ornaments were carefully hung from the branches. Most of that was done by the two adults.

As they added icicles and other finishing touches, Reed asked, "Will we put up the train?"

"I surely think so," Sam said. "We always do."

The two boys immediately worked on the train. Several minutes later, the tree decorations were finished, and the Lionel train slowly traversed its track. The family sat quietly in the room, illuminated only by tree lights and the open fireplace.

"It's so pleasant and restful," Clara said. "Now we're ready for the Christmas season."

Maybe so, Sam thought, *but I can't help wondering what kind of Christmas those servicemen around the world will have. Some won't be very pleasant.*

Sam had never felt colder. *We might as well stay in this foxhole as long as we can,* he thought. *It won't be any warmer out in the breeze.*

"First squad!" someone shouted. "Out of those holes and on your feet!"

"Oh, shit," Bernie said. "Looks like Sarge is determined to be his usual pain in the ass."

"Form up, Men!" the sergeant barked. "I've got several things to go over with you, and I wanna be able to see you, to be sure we're all on the same page."

The men formed up, though many groaned or grumbled.

"OK," the sergeant said, "here's the deal. For the time being, we're strictly defensive, and our job is to hold this area at all costs. I'm not sure how. First, we're seriously low on ammo. Nobody, and I mean nobody, is firing on full automatic. It's strictly semi. Got it?

"Next, is anyone out of K rations? OK, you two. Anybody got any extra? Good. Share with Gardner and Hopkins. After we finish, I want everyone to eat some of this crap before we head out for a little chore.

"About that chore—we aren't the only ones out of supplies. Everybody's low on everything. They'll try to resupply us by air this morning despite the lousy cloud cover and fog. One of the areas they'll try to hit is those open fields 100 yards east of us. It'll be any time after 0900. We're goin' out there and form up in the tree line to wait and watch. If we get a drop, it's our job to pull in the stuff, but we have to be careful. The Krauts will try to stop us. We move out in ten minutes."

A little while later, the troops were at the tree line.

"All right, Men," the sergeant said. 'Spread out and stay out of sight. Take advantage of any available cover. We have to wait and see if anything happens."

I hope they come through with that resupply, Sam thought. *I finished my last K ration, and I'm down to a few rounds in my M1 and two spare clips. The sound of a C47 would beat the jingle bells on Santa's sleigh for me.*

Time passed uneventfully. Except for distant, sporadic fire, there was no indication of military activity. It remained very cold. Occasionally, some of the men moved to try to keep warm.

"I think I hear somethin'!" someone shouted. "It's a plane!"

The troops, returning to the edge of the woods, scanned the cloudy skies. The sound of the planes became louder every moment and seemed right overhead, though they weren't visible. Then the sound diminished, as the planes pulled away.

"There's a parachute comin' down to the right!" a man shouted. "There's another...and more!"

"OK, Men," the sergeant called. "Get out there and pull those in. Keep your eyes open. If the Krauts open up, hit the dirt and try to get back to the trees."

Several cartons of supplies were retrieved and carried or dragged back to safety. Shouts of elation accompanied the discovery of ammunition belts, grenades, mortar rounds, and even more of the disparaged K rations.

"I'm goin' after that big one by that rock outcrop," Bernie said. "It must be somethin' special."

When he was halfway, small arms fire sounded near the farmhouse to the far left of the fields. Running, he dived to the ground beside the carton.

"Leave it, Kid!" the sergeant shouted. "Get the hell back here."

"It ain't heavy. I can make it."

Dragging the large carton, he was almost back at the tree line when a heavy machine opened up. He staggered, fell, and sprawled motionless in the snow. The nearest troops pulled him and the carton into the relative safety of the trees. A quick inspection revealed he was dead.

"Get me one of his dog tags and cover him with one of the chutes," the sergeant said.

"Huh," someone said. "There's an H on his tag. He never said anything about being Jewish. What's in the carton?"

"It's wrapping paper for Christmas presents! For Christ's sake. What asshole thought we needed that? Another headquarters SNAFU."

Sam felt sick. What quirk of fate got a Jewish boy killed trying to retrieve Christmas wrappings? There was so much waste in the war.

Sam's eyes flew open. *Oh, my God. Not another of those damn war dreams. I can't understand why I'm having them. I hope I'm not losing my mind. What time is it? It's only two-thirty. I'd better go back to sleep before I have to get up and deal with the cows.*

Seventeen

Sam walked into the waiting room. *There's more people here than when we brought Marge after Thanksgiving,* he thought. *She said she'd be here on the four forty-five. We've got a few minutes. If it isn't late, we should have plenty of time to get to Siegal's dress shop and pick up Gayle.*

On the other side of the waiting room, an elderly couple sat on a bench with a large shopping bag between them. Sam saw packages wrapped in holiday colors sticking out the top of the bag.

No doubt they'll catch the return streetcar toward Pittsburgh. Wonder who they're spending the holiday with? Children? Brothers? Sisters? Hope they don't have their holiday marred by the loss of a family serviceman. There aren't many families who don't have someone in harm's way.

A teenage boy peering out the windows toward the trolley track shouted, "I see lights! It must be the car! Here it comes!"

Most of the people in the waiting room stood. Several walked briskly toward the doors leading to the loading platform. In a few seconds, the doors were pushed open, and people flooded into the room. Most headed toward the doors leading outside, but a few were greeted with cries of delight.

Sam saw Marge walking toward him with a smile. He was about to step toward her when a young man in military uniform sprinted past Marge and grasped a young woman in his arms. Everyone in the room became silent, as the couple embraced. He stepped back with his hands on her shoulders, while tears streamed down her face.

I love you, he mouthed silently.

She shook with emotion, while those in the room began applauding. The young man looked around, smiled, nodded, and led his girlfriend from the waiting room.

Sam took Marge's suitcase, and they walked from the room.

"That was a lovely scene," Marge said. "It's a pity they aren't all coming home like that."

Sam didn't trust his voice at the moment, so he just nodded.

They walked to where the car was parked near the terminal.

"You might as well sit up front with me," Sam said. "There's plenty of room for your suitcase and Gayle in the back seat."

"I'll sit in back. Gayle's been feeling pretty low lately. I don't want her feeling like excess baggage."

"You're probably right. Hmmm. Looks like we have to contend with traffic."

"It's the last shopping day, and all the procrastinators are panicking. It was a mess in Pittsburgh."

"If we're lucky, we might find a parking spot near Siegal's, so Gayle doesn't have to walk too far. There she is on the corner. I'll pull up to the curb, so she can step right in."

In a few minutes, Sam and his two sisters were finally on their way out of town.

"Gayle, I should've asked before, but do we need to stop by your apartment for anything?" Sam asked.

"No. I've got everything I need in my train case and this shopping bag. Have you heard any news about the fighting?"

"I heard a couple news reports on the radio, and I saw the headlines on a Pittsburgh paper in the streetcar station when I waited for Marge. It's not real clear, but it could be that German drive is losing steam. Just a day or two ago, they pushed the Allies back as much as thirty-two miles. Today they said there haven't been any further advances. It has something to do with the town of Bastogne in that area. Our boys are surrounded, but the Germans haven't been able to push them out. Maybe there's a reason to be encouraged."

"I hope so."

"I suppose you were really busy at the dress shop today," Marge said, hoping to change the subject.

"Not as much as you'd think. Most of our customers buy dresses to wear, not for gifts, except for desperate men who show up at the last minute. Mostly for today we sold accessories—handbags, gloves, and scarves. We have a nice line of costume jewelry, too."

"Did they have a big layout for Christmas?"

"They had some nice decorations, but it wasn't overdone. Mr. Siegal's a Jew, so his family doesn't celebrate Christmas, but he's a smart enough businessman to know this is the big buying season."

"We're celebrating Christmas," Sam said. "Even with the war, at least we're together, and that's worth something."

Lots of cars drove both directions in the center of town, so the going was slow for a few blocks. As they left the congested downtown area and proceeded into the country, the three siblings recalled past Christmases.

It was the year after the war, Gayle thought. *That would be 1919. It was spring, maybe March, that Lon came home from the service. He was so good-looking in his uniform. It didn't matter to me that he wasn't in France fighting and spent a year-and-a-half in Oregon cutting lumber. He wasn't from around home and came from West Virginia near Moundsville. He worked at a sawmill near Sycamore, and two or three nights a week, he came to the station to hang around.*

Mama and Daddy didn't like him much. They thought he was just a drifter, but I had to have him. We ran off and got married in November and spent the first Christmas at home. I was probably pregnant by then. Lord, we couldn't keep our hands off each other those first few months. That was the best Christmas we ever had. We never had much in those twenty years, but he was my guy. It's been six years since he's been gone, and I miss him like it was yesterday.

Sam noticed a few snow flurries in the headlights, not enough to make driving difficult but enough to remind him of a trip on an earlier Christmas when he was a boy. The destination that day between Christmas and New Year's was the village of Amity to visit his grandparents. They took the train to West Amity Station and expected to see his grandfather waiting. The big surprise was that he didn't have a buggy or a surrey.

Grandfather Fonner was in a horse-drawn sleigh.

Sam sat between his grandparents, covered with a heavy blanket. A box full of heated bricks sat on the floor to keep his feet warm. It was a treat to ride along to the sound of bells from the horse's harness. His two youngest sisters and dad sat in the back seat, adding to the holiday spirit by singing. That was a treat.

He remembered hoping his grandmother would have some of his favorite jam-filled cookies, and he wasn't disappointed. Later that day, Granddad gave him a small wooden sleigh he made. That was a great day, one worth remembering. When Granddad passed away the following August, that ended their trips to Amity.

"Marge, I wonder what happened to that old sleigh Granddad had," Sam mused.

"I don't know. It was probably sold at the sale after Grandmom decided to give up the place and move with us. What made you ask?"

"No special reason. I was just thinking about some of the good times we had in Christmases past."

She smiled. "Yes, we had some really nice times, especially in the late teens and twenties before the crash."

We certainly did, Marge thought. *The Christmas that sticks out in my mind was the year I was a senior at Margaret Morrison and brought my best friend, Dorthea Grange, home with me. I never understood why a big-city girl from Chicago chose our little school. Her folks decided at the last minute to take the train to Florida to visit an aunt. Dorthea had enough money to go with them, but she didn't want to.*

There might have been a family rift. She accepted an invitation to come home with me without hesitation.

I worried a lot, but it was unnecessary, about how she'd get along with a bunch of country bumpkins. It turned out to be an adventure for her. She saw the inside of our general store and our little country church. She watched cows being milked and helped crank the churn to make butter, and many other things I always took for granted.

We went to a square dance, too, and she never lacked for partners. All the local fellows were crazy about such an attractive girl. Merle Crouser was especially smitten. A couple days after the dance, he came over in his dad's Model T to ask her for a drive.

When I later asked her how it went, she just smiled and nodded. Poor Merle enlisted right after Pearl Harbor, even though he was thirty-one or thirty-two. He was killed in North Africa. He must have been the first one we lost from around here.

Dorthea and I stayed in touch over the years with birthdays, Christmas cards, and an occasional letter. She graduated school and has been teaching at the college level all these years. She never married, so now we're both old maids. Maybe after the war, we can take a trip together.

The reminiscences of all three were rudely interrupted by the noise of the car rumbling through the covered bridge at Plum Sock.

"It's good we're just about home, Sam," Marge said. "Seems like I've been on the road all day."

"I'd guess you'd feel like that," he replied. "A couple more minutes, and we'll be there. No doubt Clara will have supper ready."

"I'm looking forward to that," Gayle said. "Nothing ever tastes the same when you cook for one. Lots of times, I'm so tired when I get home from work, I just have a sandwich or leftovers."

The car pulled into the lane.

"It's always good to come home," Marge remarked. "Look! Clara has the front porch light on. Your wreath looks really nice on the front door, Sam."

"I don't like to brag, but it *did* turn out well. I had enough cedar for two, and I put the other one on Mom and Dad's grave."

Once inside the house, they met Clara and Jimmie in the usual confusion of exchanged greetings, inquiries about health, and holiday wishes."

"Is Reed gone somewhere?" Marge asked.

"I expect he's in the barn," Sam said, "finishing the milking. Is that right, Clara?"

She nodded. "We could always count on him, but he's become a real help with everything in the last year. He worries me, though. Young folks his age think they're immortal, and he keeps hoping the war won't be over before he's old enough to enlist. I hope it doesn't happen."

The conversation paused.

"Smells like we've got something good for supper," Gayle said.

"I hope so," Clara said. "We butchered a couple weeks ago, and I've been saving a nice pork loin for a special occasion. I did it in the pressure cooker, so it should be nice and tender. We've got plenty to go with it. As soon as Reed gets in from the barn, we'll be ready to sit down."

The telephone rang.

"Was that your ring?" Marge asked.

"I believe it was." Clara went to the small table in the corner of the living room and lifted the receiver.

"Hello? Hello?" She paused. "Oh, hello, Irene. It's good to hear from you." She paused again. "When did you get word of that? How serious are the wounds? That may be a blessing if it works out the right way." She paused. "Of course you want to do that. Go right ahead, and thank you for giving us the news. Good-bye."

Clara hung up and turned to the others. "Well, that certainly was interesting. The call started out disquieting, but it may have a happy ending. That was Irene Martin. They got word that Hank, their son, was wounded in the fighting in the Philippines. It wasn't life-threatening, but she said he might be shipped home. She didn't want to talk too long, because she wanted to call other family members."

"I hope he isn't left with a disability," Gayle said. "It's strange. It seems like yesterday that he was just a little fellow who came around to see Ralph, and they'd go off to the big creek at Plum Sock to catch bluegills."

Sam said, "It seems you can't shake your head but something comes up to remind us of the horrors of this war and better times in the same blink of an eye."

"It'll be tough for some of those fellows to make the transition from being soldiers to getting back to civilian life," Marge said.

Sam nodded. "That's true, but I've been reading in the news that there's government help on the way."

"Oh? What might that be?"

"Something they're calling the GI Bill of Rights. It recognizes the sacrifices the boys have made and are still making. The idea is to give them a leg up in putting their lives back together."

"Sounds good in general. Any specifics?"

"I can't remember all of it, but there's financial help for education, like tuition and room and board for college. There was also something about low-interest loans to buy home, as well as offering health and medical benefits. Some of those fellows will come back with medical problems that'll be with them for many years."

Gayle smiled. "Neither of my boys set the world on fire with their schoolwork, so I'm not sure there's anything in that for them except the home-loan thing."

"Don't be too sure. The way I got it, some of the education funds were for craft and technical schools. They'll get the training to become electricians, plumbers, machinists, or tool and die makers. Those are good jobs, and they pay as well as or better than being a school teacher."

"Suppose we continue this conversation at the dinner table?" Clara asked. "The food won't be fit to eat if we don't get at it soon. Reed will be in from the barn almost any minute."

There was a scurry of activity, as the two aunts put their luggage and personal belongings in the bedroom where they would stay. Sam, pulling on his bib overalls and work boots, hurried out to the barn. Clara and Jimmie went into the kitchen.

Jimmie watched his mom check the pots on the stove before peeking into the oven, as Marge walked into the kitchen.

"My, it didn't take you long to get things squared away," Clara said.

"I didn't really put things away. I just dropped them on the bed, so I could come down and see if there was anything I could do to help."

"The table needs to be set, and you know where everything is. Jimmie, I'd like you to help your Aunt Marge."

Soon, they arranged plates and tableware.

"Jimmie, did you have a Christmas program at school this year?" Marge asked.

"Yes, we did. It was the last day of school in the afternoon, which was yesterday."

"Can you tell me about it?"

"Well, there was singing, reading Bible verses, recitations, and there was a little play. They called it a skit."

"That sounds nice. What part did you have?"

"I had to be in some of the singing in the large group, not a single or a duet."

"Anything else?"

"Yes. I had a recitation."

"What was it? I'd like to hear it."

"It was part of a poem by Mr. Whittier called *School Days*. The whole thing's pretty long, so I'm glad I didn't have to do it all."

"I think I remember that one. I'd like to hear you recite it
for me."

"OK."

Pushing with restless feet the snow,
To right and left he lingered.
As restlessly the tiny hands,
The blue-checked apron fingered.
He saw her lift her eyes; he felt
The soft hands light caressing
And heard the tremble of her voice,
As if a fault confessing.
I'm sorry that I spelt the word:
I hate to go above you,
Because—brown eyes lower fell—
Because, you see, I love you.

Still memory to a grey-haired man
That sweet child face is showing
Dear girl! The grasses on her grave
Have forty years been growing.
He lives to learn in life's hard school
How few who pass above him
Lament their triumph and his loss
Like her because they love him.

"Oh, my, Jimmie. What a good job. I remember that one
now. Do you know what the message of the poem is?"

"Maybe. It means that when you grow up, there's a lot of
mean people."

"Something like that. Anyway, it's a sweet poem."

Before there was a chance for further conversation, Sam and
Reed entered the kitchen from outside, and Gayle came downstairs.

"I think it's mealtime, Jimmie," Marge said.

Eighteen

"Clara, that was a great dinner," Gayle said. "It really hit the spot. Living alone, I hardly ever have a chance to fix a real meal. I usually eat whatever leftovers I can find when I get home from work."

"Glad you liked it, Gayle. I wasn't sure what to have. I didn't want to have chicken, since we'll have turkey tomorrow, so I settled on those ham slices. It didn't take them long to cook once we were back from church. There's some ham left and another whole one in the cellar from last year's butchering, plus the ones Sam just finished curing. It's not like we'll run out of ham anytime soon."

Seated at the side of the table, Reed stared intently down at his plate, struggling to keep his expression neutral. *Good Lord,* he thought. *We need more ham like a hole in the head. It seems like we have it every other day.*

"Speaking of church," Gayle said, "that was another unusual experience for me. Being on my feet and working six days a week, I usually stay in bed till noon on Sunday and take it easy the rest of the day. How about you, Marge? Are you still a churchgoer?"

"Occasionally, but it's not regular. I try to catch up on my rest, just like you. I sometimes correct papers on Sunday and deal with reports and paperwork they keep pushing on us teachers. To tell you the truth, going to a big-city church isn't like the service this morning and what we were used to while growing up. After the service this morning, folks I hadn't seen in years came up to say hello and ask how I was. Fat chance of anyone doing that in the city. They're hell bent on hopping into their cars and getting away as fast as possible."

She thought about it. "I enjoyed myself this morning. It brought back memories of when we were girls growing up before Mom and Dad died. I remember those good times."

The three women were lost in memories of past holidays. The quiet was broken by a loud snort.

"What in the world was that?" Gayle asked.

Clara laughed. "That was Sam. I recognize his snoring. He lay on the sofa in the parlor right after dinner, and he must've fallen asleep. He has long days even on Sunday. You can't take a day off from milking."

"Did the boys go up for a nap, too?"

"Oh, no. Not those two. Reed left to walk back to the church to meet his friends. They plan to play Ping-Pong in the church basement. Jimmie went to check his traps."

"Traps? I didn't know anyone still did that."

"Oh, a few of the youngsters do. There isn't much reward for their effort, though. Jimmie tried it for the first time last year, and I think he had five skunk hides by the end of the season. They were all number four, so his total take was around a dollar and a quarter."

"Skunk? That must've been quite a mess."

"Not really. He was lucky. He got close enough to see a couple were still alive in the trap and came back to get Reed or Sam to take care of them with the twenty-two. Sam thinks Jimmie's a little young to take the gun by himself.

"Some of the other young fellows weren't as lucky. I talked to Jimmie's teacher awhile ago. She said when they were at the old one-room school, on really cold days when the pot-bellied coal burner was going strong, it baked the skunk smell out of the boys' pants and jackets until she smelled it on her own clothes. You don't have that problem, do you, Marge?"

"No, thank the Lord. A lot of those city kids wouldn't know a skunk even if they tripped over it."

"By the way, Clara, who were those folks you talked to so long after church?"

"George and Rose Snyder. They live down near Deer Lick. They don't come to church that often, so I hadn't seen them in quite a while."

"I know who you're talking about," Gayle said. "They live down near the old Snyder place. Lon worked with him on that rig-building crew when they drilled those wells on the Weir farm. He wasn't on that casing job when George was hurt."

"That was an awful thing. It laid George up for the better part of a year. To be honest, he never got back to the way he'd been before the accident. They had a tough time of it. If Frank hadn't been there to keep the farm going, I don't know what would have happened."

"Who's Frank?" Marge asked. "I didn't think they had kids."

"They don't. Frank Kozloski showed up in the spring of the year before George was hurt. He was on the bum like lots of fellows during the thirties. I believe he came from hard-coal country in the northern part of the state. He stopped by to ask if he could do some work for a meal. Rose gave him a few jobs to do and was impressed at how good he was. I don't remember the details, but one thing led to another, and he stayed on for over two years and worked for room and board. He was a nice young fellow. Everyone liked him, and he was a hard worker. Rose and George took to him like the son they never had."

"What happened to him?"

"The year before Pearl Harbor, after George recovered as much as he could, Frank decided to do something for himself and enlisted in the Army. Rose and George hated seeing him go, but they understood he couldn't spend his life working for food and a place to stay."

"Now what?"

"He's done pretty well for himself. Rose said he was recently promoted to Master Sergeant, and he's stationed in Australia, doing something with aerial photographs. Rose showed me pictures of him he sent. He's a real handsome fellow in his uniform. They're as proud of him as if he were kin. They keep hoping he won't be sent into combat and get hurt or worse."

"I have to say, Clara, it's nice to hear a feel-good story for once. That's put me in the mood to go upstairs and lie down for a nap."

"That's fine. What about you, Gayle? Is it your siesta time, too?"

"No. I haven't written to Rex since earlier this week. I want to do that, and I'll send a note to a couple of people who wrote me a few lines in their Christmas cards."

"All right. You two go ahead. I want to mix the stuffing for the turkey. I'll stuff the bird after supper, so we don't have as much to do tomorrow morning."

"I don't expect to nap for long," Marge said. "I'll be back down after a bit to help with supper."

"Supper won't require much. I'm planning on a pot of potato soup and sandwiches. I've got cold cuts and cheese from the store, and there's chocolate cake for dessert."

Jimmie walked down the road before stepping off toward the creek. A couple places along the bank looked like they might be muskrat holes, so he secured traps there. He found them empty.

Maybe I'll get one in a day or two, he thought.

He continued walking beside the stream and soon reached the old school where he attended his first four years. It looked the same as it had when it was closed the previous year.

He walked onto the porch and saw a padlock securing the door, then he tried the hand pump on the porch without success. At the back of the building was the coal shed and two privies he remembered.

What'll they ever do with this old place? he wondered.

Leaving the area of the school building, he walked up the gentle, wooded slope to the left that served as a playground. The trees varied in size from saplings to mature. All lost their leaves, which covered the ground.

Near the top of the slope was the level, graded area of the railroad track bed. Just below that was the foxhole he and his friends dug out. He smiled when he saw the remains of the make-believe machine gun Sam made for him with a piece of rain spout. He remembered the times they fantasized about repelling enemy forces.

He forgot about his other traps, as he walked along the rail line. Soon, he came to the place where a red dog road crossed. He stopped, trying to decide whether to continue or go home, when his thoughts were interrupted by the sound of a car coming along the road to his right. It sounded like it was going faster than Sam ever drove on those back roads.

As the car neared, he saw it belonged to Mr. Thomas from Plum Sock. Jimmie was surprised when the car stopped near him, and the driver rolled down the window.

"Hi, there! I believe it's Jimmie Minor. How you doing, Boy?"

Jimmie recognized the driver as Glenn Thomas, a few years older than Reed, in a Navy uniform. Seated beside him in the front seat was a young woman.

"Hi, Glenn. I'm OK. I didn't know you were in the service."

With the window open, the odor of tobacco smoke and something else—perhaps beer or whiskey—floated out.

"Yep," Glenn said. "Uncle Sam got me last summer soon after I graduated from high school. They let me come home for a few days after boot camp. Next Wednesday, I'm going to Norfolk, and they'll put me on a boat. Wanda, I've got a terrible thirst. Would you hand me that bottle?"

Jimmie watched the young woman hand Glenn a brown bottle, who gulped down some of the contents. Jimmie didn't recognize the woman. She had blonde hair and bright-red lipstick.

"Ah," Glenn said. "That hit the spot. Well, Boy, I expect you're getting ready for Santy Claus. What will he bring you tonight?"

"I don't know. Probably some clothes."

"Huh? Well, Wanda here is very patriotic and a big supporter of the war effort. I got an early Christmas present from her last night, and I didn't need no clothes. I'm expectin' another present, maybe two, tonight to boost my morale before I go off to do my duty."

The woman giggled. "Glenn, Honey, you shouldn't talk that way in front of the boy!"

"Gotta be going, Jimmie. Don't take any wooden nickels." The wheels spun, and stones flew as the car roared away.

Jimmie wondered about the encounter, as he walked toward home. A few years later, he would understand the nature of the conversation.

Reed felt warm from his exertions. It was the third game in a row. When they arrived at the church and went into the basement in the early afternoon, it was very chilly and a bit musty. There was the faint aroma of past church suppers. The furnace was on during church and Sunday school earlier in the day, but it didn't provide heat for the basement other than whatever seeped around the doorframe into the furnace room. They lit the gas-fired space heater, and, in the ensuing two hours, the room temperature rose significantly.

He was well ahead with a score of 16-20. *I'd like to get this over with,* he thought.

Bill returned the ball to Reed's right, which enabled him to get under it and add plenty of spin to his return. As he hoped, the ball squirted off to Bill's left and wasn't returnable.

"OK," Reed said. "I don't know about you guys, but I've had enough for today."

He checked his watch. "Anyway, it's just shy of three, and I have to get down the road. It'll soon be time to pull tits."

"Why don't you hang around awhile?" Claude asked. "We were going to see if Nancy Smith was home. She's always ready for a walk somewhere. It's a more than better chance to get your hands on real tits. She's almost always ready to play."

"Nancy? Oh, my God. You've got to be kidding. She's ugly as sin."

Claude laughed. "Hell, you don't have to look at her. Anyway, her tits aren't ugly. Last time I went over there, she played with my pecker. I had a big handful for her. Sure you don't want to try for some?"

"Nope. You can have her all to yourself. I'm headin' down the road. Bill, you coming?"

"Yeah, I guess so."

As the two boys walked outside, Reed glanced up at the cemetery on the hill behind the church, remembering being up there the fall before Pearl Harbor, when they buried his granddad. *What a day that was. All those people who showed up at home for the funeral until the house was packed, then people sat outside on the front and side porches. All those cars following the hearse up here, with most folks coming back to the house to eat and visit. I don't much care for funerals.*

Reed and Bill began their trek toward their homes. It was a crisp, overcast winter afternoon.

"Do you think what they said about Nancy was true, or were they just bullshittin'?" Bill asked.

"They might've been puffin' up the story a bit, but that's not the first time I've heard stories about Nancy being free and easy. Where there's smoke, there's fire. Trouble with that, though, is 'fore long, somebody's gonna get her knocked up, and then there'll be a shotgun wedding. Ugh. Wouldn't you hate to think of spending the rest of your life looking at her ugly puss every day?"

Reed looked at Bill. "You gonna have a big feed at your place tomorrow?"

"No. After we open presents, we'll drive down to Waynesburg to my sister Donna's place. She'll have the meal for us. Her husband got a furlough, and he's home from where he's stationed in Fort Meade, somewhere near Washington, DC. He's an officer, but I don't know what he does. It's something about intelligence. Maybe I'll find out tomorrow."

"I guess he isn't from around here. How'd she ever hook up with him?"

"They were in college at State together. He was in a military thing—ROTC or something—and the military paid for some of his college. Now he has to serve for a while. They got married right after graduation, but then the following December, we had Pearl Harbor. He's been in ever since. Donna's scared to death he'll have to go overseas and fight."

He looked up. "Reed, this is where I turn off. Have a nice Christmas. See you."

"You, too."

Nineteen

Sam and the two boys came into the kitchen from outside.

"The milking is over, Clara," Sam said. "Supper about ready?"

"Yes. The soup's ready. I just have to set the table and get out the other things from the fridge onto the table. Take off your outside things and wash up. Reed, if you're going upstairs, would you tell your aunts we're about ready to eat?"

Jimmie, hanging up his coat, struggled to remove his boots. He leaned back in his chair when he finished and looked around the kitchen, which was warm and damp, with all the windows coated with moisture. Clara used a spoon to taste the soup and smiled with a nod. She picked up a cigarette from the edge of the small marble-topped cabinet beside the stove and took a drag. The junk room door opened, and Sam stepped out.

"I can see by the big grin on your face that you and Mr. Seagram's had a little encounter in there," Clara said.

"You don't miss much, do you?" He chuckled.

"It's a pretty rare occasion when you take a snort, so it stands out. I'm just kidding. We won't have to call in the WCTU any time soon. You've been working on that pint bottle for a year and a half."

A few minutes later, Reed, Marge, and Gayle came into the kitchen.

"Anything we can do to help?" Marge asked.

"Why don't you take the plates and table settings into the dining room? Gayle can help me take up the soup and get the sandwich makings, and then we'll be ready to eat."

Soon, all the family sat around the dining room table, and Sam busily ladeled soup.

"Clara, you outdid yourself with this soup," Gayle said. "I can't remember when I've had anything that tasted this good."

Marge added, "Oscar would have really liked this. Potato soup was his all-time favorite."

"Who's Oscar?" Jimmie asked.

"He was the hired man at our farm, Oscar Mueller. He was the farm manager. He worked here for a number of years until he left sometime in the midthirties. You remember him, don't you, Reed?"

"I think so. He was a tall man with a big mustache, and he spent a lot of time around the horses when we still had some. He talked kinda funny, right?"

"That describes him pretty well. Gayle, remember how he liked Christmas? On Christmas Eve, after dinner, he came downstairs with his concertina and tried to teach us German Christmas carols without much success. Anyone remember what they were?"

"I can help with that," Sam said. "I didn't know them at the time, but I had to take some German in college, and it came back to me. His favorites were *Stille Nacht* and *O Tannenbaum*. We recognized the tunes, but the German was more than we could handle. The first was *Silent Night*. The second was *O Fir Tree*. It's to the tune of *Oh, Christmas Tree*."

"Christmas Eve was the only time I can remember Oscar trying to sing with us," Marge added.

"The time of year might have made him recall his youth in Germany. Maybe he had an extra shot of schnapps to mark the occasion."

"Schnapps! That's hard to believe. Mother would never have allowed alcohol in the house."

"Huh. Sis, you forget what a sweet and trusting person Mom was, even a little naïve. We all knew Pop had a drink now and then, but she was sure he never had. The truth is, Pop kept a bottle in the barn somewhere. He got schnapps for Oscar occasionally."

"Seems like I'm getting an education tonight," Marge said. "He left us in the midthirties. Whatever happened to him?"

"He went to live with a niece near Pittsburgh somewhere. He wanted to be with family, even though he lived for only a couple more years. He heard from other family members across the water. He was proud of his heritage, but he once told me he didn't like what he heard from that Hitler fellow, and he thought there would be trouble."

"He was a good prophet about that."

"Sam, speaking of Germans and Germany," Gayle asked, "have you heard any news today about the fighting over there?"

"Some, not a lot. We don't get the paper on Sunday, and the regular news commentators aren't working Sunday, either. I talked to Frank at church, and they get a Pittsburgh paper delivered. There was some good news that the weather cleared a bit, so our planes were back in business. They've been hitting enemy positions and were able to drop food, ammunition, and supplies to the soldiers who were cut off and surrounded in Bastogne. Maybe our guys can go on the offensive before long."

He paused. "There was something else, not about the fighting, but it's important to the war effort. They're saying the Sixth War Bond Drive that ended a week ago was a big success. They got something over twenty-one million, almost twice the goal. It's hard to imagine that amount of money."

"Well," Clara said, "it's getting late. Let's clear the table. I have a couple things to do, and I'd like to spend some time just sitting in the parlor and looking at the Christmas tree."

After supper, each of the family members had a special activity to do alone. Sam slept in his favorite chair in the living room, and Clara stuffed the turkey for Christmas dinner. Marge found family photo albums in the living room cupboard and spread them out on the dinner table. As she leafed through the pages, she occasionally chuckled or commented.

Reed was in the bedroom, studying his matchbook collection. Jimmie, feeling restless, tried to find something that would help the time pass quickly. When he heard a piano playing, he knew where to find his other aunt.

He walked into the parlor and saw Gayle repeatedly striking one key. She looked up at him and shook her head.

"There's no hope for that note, Jimmie," she said. "It's dead as a doornail."

"Are you going to play something?"

"I can try. What would you like to hear?"

"How about *Jingle Bells?* Should I look for the songbook?"

"I don't read music. I just play by ear." She struck a few chords and began playing. "Sing with me, Jimmie."

Jingle bells, jingle bells, jingle all the way
Oh, what fun it is to ride in a one-horse open sleigh

They repeated the verse several times, then she stopped playing.

"Aunt Gayle, did you know we have two old sleighs in the barn?" he asked. "They're way high up on a platform near the roof. Dad must've used the hay fork to get them up there. Did you ever ride in a sleigh?"

"I did several times when I was a little girl. Chances are, it was one of those in the barn. When I was growing up, the roads weren't paved, so when we had a big snow, a sleigh was the only way to get around."

"Wasn't it awful cold?"

"Sometimes, but we'd get all bundled up and covered up with a blanket. Sometimes, Mama heated bricks in the stove and put them in a box on the floor of the sleigh. That really kept our feet warm.

"It always seemed like a big adventure. They had special harness for the horses, with small bells on it that rang, as we traveled. That's where *Jingle Bells* came from."

She played a few bars of another song, then stopped and looked aside as if thinking of something. She started playing again, stopped, and continued.

"I recognize that," Jimmie said. "What is it? It's *White Christmas.*"

Gayle hummed along for a while, then stopped to retrieve a handkerchief from the front of her dress to dab at her eyes.

"What's wrong, Aunt Gayle?"

"I'm just being a silly old woman. The words of the song reminded me of some of the nice Christmas times I had in the past, like when I was a little girl and later when my boys were your age. I can't help wondering what kind of Christmas they're having this year. Chances are it's not very nice."

Jimmie didn't know what to say. He couldn't remember ever seeing an adult cry, and it made him uncomfortable. As Gayle continued playing, he left the parlor.

Sometime later, Clara walked in and was surprised no one was there. *Sam's still napping in the living room, and it seems everyone else went to bed,* she thought. *It's nice to have a little time to myself. Today was pretty hectic, and tomorrow will be more of the same.*

She settled comfortably at the end of the sofa and alternated her view between the tree lights and the glimmering coals in the fireplace. Just as her eyes began to feel heavy, Marge came into the room.

"I thought maybe you turned in for the night," Clara said.

"No. I was reading a novel that came out earlier this year, and, while my eyes got tired, I wasn't sleepy. I decided to come down and see if anyone was still up."

"What were you reading?"

"It's called *The Razor's Edge,* and it's about a fellow who was a pilot in the big war and had some tough experiences. He tried to get his mind straightened out. It's interesting, but it's not an easy read, and you really have to concentrate."

"I used to read when I was younger, but I can't seem to find the time anymore."

"Huh. Us old maids don't have husbands and kids to keep us busy around the clock. We've got plenty of free time on our hands."

"It's nice to have a little time on Christmas Eve to relax, and, as Sam likes to say, charge your batteries."

"There's certainly a lot of hard work keeping things going on a farm."

"That's so, but it's only part of it. The other thing is the war. It seems like every time you turn around, you're hit by another aspect of it. Somebody just got drafted, sent overseas, was wounded, captured, or killed. Or we get new food-rationing cards or gas cards. Things we used to buy if we had the money can't be had at any price. They simply aren't available. I've been starting to feel like I'm being worn down. A month ago, it seemed like the end was in sight, at least in Europe, but now, who knows? We take one step forward and two steps back.

"On top of it all, I'm scared to death it won't be over by the time Reed's old enough for the draft. I don't know if they're running out of manpower or what, but the news last week said they'll start drafting men in the twenty-six to thirty-eight age group starting February first if their jobs aren't critical."

"I wish I had answers for you, Clara, but I don't. Mama used to say it's always darkest before the dawn. Maybe we can hope the end is just around the corner."

The two women sat silently for several minutes. Finally, Clara stood.

"I'm turning in, Marge," she said. "Morning will come pretty early, and we have a lot to do. Merry Christmas."

"To you, too, Clara."

Twenty

Jimmie awoke and opened his eyes. Except for the illumination from the hall light through the crack in the door, it was pitch dark. He wondered what time it was, and then he realized it was Christmas day. Pulling the blanket away from the side of his face, he listened intently.

There aren't any sounds, he thought. *Nobody else must be awake and moving. It won't hurt to get some clothes on and go downstairs to look at the tree.*

A few minutes later, he pulled on his pants and shirt in the bathroom. Carrying his shoes, he carefully walked downstairs. At the bottom, he stopped to listen again.

No sounds. Guess I didn't wake anybody. I'll put on my shoes and take a look, but there probably won't be much. All the presents will be wrapped, and we don't unwrap them until after breakfast. When Mom thought I still believed in Santa Claus, she always left some unwrapped.

He walked into the parlor. The tree lights were left on all night, so there was light in the room. Feeling the cool air, he walked to the fireplace and put a piece of wood on the coals. With a few thrusts with the poker, the fire ignited along the wood, and he turned to look at the presents under the tree.

Whoa! What's that box that isn't wrapped? he wondered.

He knelt and saw pictures on the box showing a battleship being torpedoed by a submarine.

This has gotta be for me. It's with the others that have my name on the tags. Let's see what it's about.

He opened the box and took out several wooden items, noticing the underside of the box top had diagrams that showed how to fit the pieces together.

I see how this works. The two big pieces fit together to make an enemy ship. Oh! There's a target on one side and a spring that'll make a part fly off when you hit the target. The small one's like a submarine. It has a spring and a trigger. You can shoot wooden torpedoes at the target. I have to try it out.

In moments, he assembled the toy and lay on the floor to take aim at the enemy ship. His first two shots missed, but the third one was accurate, and the ship flew apart.

Wow! That was neat! Let's put it together and try again.

Occupied by the new toy, he hit the target and moved farther back to try again. He was so absorbed, he didn't hear Sam walk in.

"Looks like your aim's pretty good," Sam said.

"Hi, Dad. I'm learning. This is great fun. You have to hit it just right to make the ship explode."

"I'm glad you like it, but try not to make too much noise. No one else is up yet. I'm going into the kitchen to fix coffee and something to eat."

Jimmie played with the toy for a few more minutes, but his eyes grew heavy, and he began yawning. He curled up on the sofa and fell asleep in moments.

Clara walked into the kitchen and toward the stove. She smiled, as she lifted the coffee pot.

"I'm glad you made coffee, Sam. I need a boost, and I wouldn't have wanted to wait until a new pot perked."

She poured a cup for herself, sat at the table, and lit a cigarette.

"That will help me get going." She exhaled a cloud of smoke. "I guess you noticed Jimmie is up?"

"Yes. He was up when I came down. I looked in on him awhile ago, and he was fast asleep on the sofa, clutching that boat like he was afraid it would get away. What's your plan for today?"

"The turkey's stuffed, and, as soon as breakfast is over, I'll stick it in the oven. After we open presents, I start on the rest of the meal. Marge and Gayle will help, so it won't be too bad. I'll stir the buckwheat cake batter after I finish my coffee. Would you get one of those small crocks of baked sausage from the milk house, and I'll be ready for breakfast when the rest get down there?"

"All right. By the way, what's for dessert?"

"I have twenty-four-hour salad for the meal, and I made hickory nut cake. How does that sound?"

"OK. It suits me, but when will we ever have one of those pecan pies you make so well?"

"Not this month. We don't have much sugar left, and we've used all our ration coupons for the month. We used a lot for cookies and candy over the last few weeks."

Clara and Sam turned their heads, as they heard someone come downstairs and walk through the living room. Gayle entered the kitchen.

"Have some coffee, Gayle," Clara said. "I'm making a fresh pot. Did you sleep well?"

"Indeed, I did. I guess my body knew it was back home. That coffee will hit the spot."

The morning passed quickly, as various family members woke and came down for breakfast. The last was Reed, perhaps hoping to appear adult and in disdain for the holiday that was oriented for children. Opening presents brought excitement, because there were surprises. The boys' ice skates were unexpected, and Reed was genuinely pleased.

Jimmie was thrilled to get the book *Red Randall at Midway.* "I know this will be really neat! I liked the other Red Randall books

I got earlier this year for my birthday. One was about Red Randall at Pearl Harbor."

Most of the gifts were clothing. Sam received dress shirts and neckties for teaching, and Jimmie was excited to receive his first long pants.

Clara feigned surprise at her gift from Jimmie. "What in the world can this be?" She continued unwrapping it. "Oh, my goodness! A nice round mirror for the table centerpiece. That will look very nice."

Marge brought wrapped gifts she received from friends. "I always save my gift from Dorthea for last. She always gives me something really nice."

I suppose that means she doesn't expect anything nice from us, Clara thought. *Damn her. I guess two old maids without any real responsibilities would be able to give each other nice gifts.*

When all the presents were unwrapped, the process was over until the next year.

"Everyone did fairly well," Clara said. "I have to get back to the kitchen. There's a lot to be done to have the meal ready on time."

The household was busy for two-and-a-half hours. As the smell of the cooking turkey became more pervasive, kitchen activities intensified. Jimmie played with his new war-oriented toy, and Reed examined the skates in detail and tried them on. Sam made frequent trips into the kitchen to gauge the meal progress. Between times, he listened to the radio in a futile search for news reports. Finally, the preparations for Christmas dinner were finished, and the male family members were summoned to the dining room.

When all were seated, Clara offered a brief prayer. In deference to Gayle, she omitted any mention of the war and servicemen. All turned their attention to Sam at the end of the table, as he carved the turkey. In a few moments, plates full of generous helpings sat before all the diners.

When the feast was over, the boys were excused from the dining room, and the adults sat to have after-meal cigarettes.

Reed returned to the dining room. "Dad, a car just drove into the lane."

"That's strange on Christmas Day," Sam said. "Do you recognize it?"

"Can't say I do."

Sam stood and peered out through the bubbles in the antique glass windows. "It's familiar, but I can't place it. Oh, that's Tip Grim, one of the road supervisors, coming up the walk. Wonder what he wants."

Sam walked to the door and put his hand on the knob. When Tip knocked, Sam opened the door.

"Come on in, Tip. What brings you out on a holiday?"

"Nothing good, as you might guess. I tried to call you, but the operator couldn't connect with your Farmers Company."

"Probably a line down somewhere. It happens all the time, then all we get are local calls. We've done everything but get down on our knees and beg to get the Bell people to take over and modernize the company without any luck. I understand over 100,000 people are still waiting for phones. Nothing's gonna happen until the war's over, but I'm sure you didn't stop by to discuss the phone. What's up?"

Tip's expression turned somber. "There's been an accident, with a couple people killed. There are complications I don't know how to handle. I thought you might have an idea."

"I'll help if I can. First, I want you two, Reed and Jimmie, to go into the parlor, so Tip and I can have a private conversation."

The boys reluctantly left the room.

"Sometime last night," Tip explained, "a car ran off the road on that curve just before the covered bridge by the Andrews place. It ended upside down in five feet of water in the creek. We don't know when it happened. Dorsey Smith spotted it at ten o'clock on his way to his brother's place and came right over to tell me. The boys and I took the Allis Chambers and a log chain. It was a hell of a job, but we finally got it out.

"We found two bodies inside. I recognized the man, not more than a boy, right off, as being Glenn Thomas. I heard he was home on leave from the service. Then I realized it was his daddy's car. I didn't recognize the woman, but Wayne, my older son, did. He said her name's Wanda Crawford, and she lived near Nineveh somewhere.

"I didn't know what to do with the bodies. I called the state cops, but when I said the two were dead, they said they didn't see any point driving all the way out here, bein' as they're short-handed on Christmas Day. The telephone operator was some help and was able to get hold of the woman's family. They're sending an undertaker to get the body.

"Old Man Thomas wasn't very interested. He said he couldn't afford to bury anybody, and anyway, Glenn belonged to the Navy, so they could bury him. He seemed more concerned about his car.

"I don't know what to do. What if he's right, and this is the Navy's job? How do I find out? I sure didn't know this was part of bein' elected road supervisor."

Sam rubbed his chin for a few seconds. "Tip, I don't know if that's the Navy's job or not. The best thing I can think of is for you to contact the congressman. I don't know him myself, but his name's Grant Furlong, and he lives down by Donora along the Monongahela. He didn't get reelected, but he's still congressman until next week. He should be able to find out who to contact.

"If it's not the Navy's job, call the coroner in at the courthouse. It'll be up to the county to bury him in potter's field. I'd say use our phone, but you probably can't call out."

"Yeah. We're on Bell, and that's usually pretty good. I'll get on home and try to make those calls. I sure thank you for your help. I didn't know what to do, but Minerva, my wife, said you always were the smartest kid at school, so you'd know what to do."

"That's nice of her to say, though my teachers might not agree. One thing I'm curious about, but I doubt anyone knows the answer. What caused the accident? That's not much of a curve, and Glenn had to be familiar with the road. Was it icy up there?"

"No, it wasn't." He stared at the floor and shook his head. "All I can tell you is there was a whiskey bottle in the car, and there wasn't much left in it. That might have something to do with it. I'm not gonna say."

"You have to feel sorry for these young fellows, Tip. They go off to war and don't know if they're coming back in one piece. I guess I can understand if they want to cram in a lifetime of experiences before they go. It's a shame it has to end this way."

"That's so. Well, Sam, I have to get moving. I'll make those calls. Thanks again for the help."

They shook hands, and Tip opened the front door and left the house. At the sound of the door closing, Reed and Jimmie quickly emerged from the parlor, curiosity written on their faces.

"Well, look who's nosey," Sam said. "Come into the dining room. I don't want to tell this yarn twice."

They walked into the dining room, and Sam summarized the conversation with Tip. He didn't mention the possibility that alcohol might have played a part in the accident and the seeming indifference of Glenn's father to his son's death. The rest of the family was surprised when Jimmie suddenly spoke up.

"I saw Glenn and some girl yesterday up by the schoolhouse when I was checking my traps."

"How'd that happen?" Clara asked.

"I was up above the school, where the railroad tracks cross the road, and they came drivin' by. He stopped to say a couple words."

"Like what?"

"I dunno. It was kinda dumb. He talked about his girl. What was her name? Oh, yeah, Wanda, I think, saying she gave him his Christmas present the night before."

The adults were speechless for a moment. Sam cleared his throat, and Reed covered his grin with one hand. Jimmie glanced around with a questioning look.

Aunt Marge broke the silence. "Sam, did you say the girl's name was Crawford? I might have known her mother. She's about my age. There was talk about her, too. I guess the apple didn't fall that far from the tree."

"Well," Gayle said, "the girl's gone, and so is Glenn. We need to remember them in our prayers."

"This whole business sure puts a sour note on Christmas," Clara said. "It's time to clean up. Jimmie, you should go to your room and take a nap. We're going to Uncle Lou's for supper, so it'll be a long day."

It was fully dark by the time they gathered in the car and drove to Sam's brother's house. The annual Christmas-night trek became a tradition in recent years. It took some work on everyone's part to fit six people into the two-door Ford sedan. No one complained, though Reed wasn't very happy sharing the back seat with his two aunts. Jimmie was comfortable between his parents in the front seat, with the minor inconvenience of having to straddle the gear shift.

"Here we go," Sam said. "My food seems to have digested from earlier in the day. If not, maybe I'll hit a few bumps and pack it down. By the way, Clara, I fell asleep pretty quick after eating this afternoon. You talked about calling Grace. Were you able to catch her?"

"Yes, I did. We had a nice long chat. They had a nice Christmas, since it was the first year they've actually had two nickels to rub together. They had a few gifts for the girls, who were thrilled. The only sour note was that Larry developed a severe belly ache after they ate, and it hadn't completely cleared up by the time we talked. Grace was concerned. He's had a couple similar episodes in the last month."

"He's a young fellow," Sam said. "You wouldn't think it'd be anything serious."

The trip was very scenic, even at night. The moon was almost full, and its reflection on the light covering of snow on the fields illuminated the landscape. As they passed individual houses, interior lights and occasional colored holiday lights added accents to the winter scene. The road was mostly free of ice and snow, so it was a quick, uneventful trip.

They reached their destination, entered the house, and were immediately immersed in the holiday atmosphere. The sound of adults exchanging greetings mingled with the excited cries of Lou and Bonnie's three children, along with the removal of outer wear, created some confusion. A hint of wood smoke from the fireplace and the lingering scent of pine from the Christmas tree competed with the odor of cloves from the cooked ham. Soon, people segregated into different groups. Sam and Lou sat in the sofa to talk, as did the women in the dining room. The youngsters corralled Jimmie to show him their presents. Reed was left to himself, but he found an easy chair near the fireplace and a large supply of *Life* magazines to read.

"Don't you think my doll's nice, Jimmie?" Opal asked.

Jimmie knew that good manners required an affirmative reply, so he assured her the doll was very nice, but he was more interested in her brother's Lincoln Logs.

"Those are like mine, Billy, though I think your set has more pieces."

"Have you heard any war news?" Sam asked Lou, sitting on the far side of the room from the kids.

"Yes, I did. After we opened presents, I ran into town for milk that Bonnie needed, and I picked up a Pittsburgh paper. It's over by where Reed's sitting. You're welcome to read it. Generally, the news is good. You must've heard that the weather cleared in the last couple days, and the Air Force is knocking the hell out of the German positions. Our boys started a counterattack today on a twenty-five-mile front, and they're pushing the Krauts back. Looks like the tide's turning our way."

"That's good news. I'm sure there are plenty of tough days ahead until they get 'em pushed back to where they were before the offensive started. I'm afraid there'll be thousands of casualties on both sides."

Clara and Bonnie talked in the dining room, mostly about Christmas gifts, the dinner at the Minors, and, to some extent, the tragedy of the auto crash of the Thomas man and his companion. Soon, however, talk shifted to more-mundane things.

"Have you gotten your new food ration stamps yet, Bonnie?" Clara asked. "I believe they go into effect tomorrow."

"Yes, I did, but the changes didn't amount to much. They're emphasizing to destroy the old stamps or tokens, so people don't try to use them." Bonnie stood. "Speaking of food, it's time we got started. I won't chase anyone off, but, if it starts to snow, everyone will want to head home."

She turned to the rest of the room. "OK, Everyone! Grab a plate and help yourself. If you can't find a seat at the table, sit wherever you're comfortable."

In a few minutes, they were enjoying their second feast of the day. Afterward, the balance of the evening was devoted to conversation. Twice that night, neighbors dropped by to offer holiday greetings.

By nine o'clock, Bonnie and Lou's two older children were quarrelling about the ownership of a book. It was also clear Jimmie and the other youngster were struggling to stay awake.

"It's time we brought this evening to a close," Clara said. "It's been a long day, especially for the young folks."

No one disagreed, and Reed silently thought, *Thank God.*

"Sam, I'll be glad to take Gayle to town to her apartment," Lou offered. "It's no problem, and that'll save you some time getting home."

Sam nodded. "I appreciate that, Lou."

As they left, Marge said, "Let's hope at this time next year, we're together again with this awful war over, and our boys back home."

"Amen," Gayle said.

On the homeward-bound trip, the full moon was higher in the sky than when they left home, and the reflection on the snow gave greater illumination of the landscape.

"It seems as bright as midday," Sam said.

"Yes," Clara said. "It's so pretty, for a minute, you forget how cold it is. Did you notice we haven't passed a car going in either direction since we left Lou and Bonnie's?"

"You're right. Everybody stays close to home on Christmas."

Two miles from home, they rounded a curve and were startled to see a deer in the middle of the road. Sam slammed on the brakes to avoid hitting the creature. The deer bounded away and was soon out of sight.

"Holy cow!" Jimmie exclaimed. "That was close!"

"I didn't know we had any deer around here," Marge said.

"You see one once in a while," Sam said, "but they're pretty rare. Chances are it's not the same one you saw by the pines the other day, Jimmie."

A few minutes later, the family reached home without further excitement.

Twenty-One

Two days later, the family sat at the dining room table for their mid-day meal. Sam, the last one to join them, came in from outside.

"It's not quite as cold today as the last two," he said. "I was able to get the last two covers on the cattle sheds fixed. We should be all set if we get some big snows in the next couple months."

"You always said those Herefords were pretty tough beef stock," Reed said. "Do they really need shelter?"

"Oh, they're tough all right, and most would be content in the weather, but there are always a few frail ones. More to the point, we have calves coming soon. A little protection would be good for them."

"It's nice we have all this time off before we return to school next week," Jimmie said. "It's kind of like a winter vacation."

Sam grinned. "I'll be sure to remind the milk cows about that this evening."

"Oh. I forgot about that."

"That's all right. It's nice not to be a school teacher and part-time farmer simultaneously. It gives me a chance to catch up on some of the little things I've been wanting to do."

"What might those be?" Marge asked.

"I'd like to cut some sumacs to make spouts to tap the sugar maple trees. In a couple of months, the sap will be rising."

"Will it be necessary again this year?" Clara asked.

"It can't hurt, and we might need it if the war and the sugar rationing continues. It won't cost anything but some firewood to boil it down, and Lord knows, we've got no shortage of that."

Sam paused. "I have a mind to make some spare pitman bars for the mowing machine. I got a big piece of ash at the sawmill last spring, and it was well-cured come fall. I took it to the school, and the shop teacher roughed out pieces for me. I need to trim them up and bore holes for the connecting bolts. I usually break a couple a year if I hit rocks or a wheel falls into a hole, and it's costly to buy them. It's hard to find anything in the way of farm machinery. Seems like the only stuff being made has to do with supplies and equipment for the military.

"I'll enjoy having a few days off from teaching, but there are always things to do around a farm. Right now, I'm going to the living room to turn on the radio and see if there's a noon news report."

After the usual static and other unpleasant sounds, Sam tuned in the desired station and heard a beer commercial, then the network news came on.

"The war news from the European theater, as reported by the Associated Press, is encouraging. The Allied counteroffensive launched on Christmas Day in Belgium has picked up momentum. The success of the ground forces has been enhanced by good weather conditions, which enabled Air Force fighters and bombers to hammer German positions and supply lines.

"General George S. Patton's Third Army attacking from the south has relieved the previously surrounded forces in the city of Bastogne, which for over a week fended off almost-continuous attacks from five German divisions. Patton's forces, combined with Allied units attacking from the north, squeezed the German salient into Belgium to less than twenty miles at its narrowest point.

"The ordeal of the last two weeks has been replete with numerous stories of grit and courage exhibited by American troops. None were more striking than the response of General A. C. McAuliff, commander of the beleaguered forces in Bastogne, to the German ultimatum to surrender. His one-word answer was, 'Nuts.'

"Elsewhere, Soviet forces continue their thrust into western Hungary and appear poised to encircle the capitol city of Budapest."

It's good to have positive news, Sam thought. *I have to wonder what these successes have cost us. How many more young fellas won't come home? One has to wonder how many more battles there will be before this thing is over. It'll be tough sledding in the Pacific, as we go from island to island. Those Japs are tough. I hope the big shots know what they're doing letting the ones who live on the West Coast leave the internment camps and go home. That's risky.*

Reed opened the workshop door and stepped inside. "Wow! It sure is hot in here."

Sam looked up from his work. "Yes, it is, but this old space heater doesn't have any controls. It's a choice between hot and cold. What brings you out here?"

"I ran out of things to do at the house. I had a little schoolwork, but that's done. There isn't anything to read, so I got the willies sittin' around. I see you're working on those pitman bars for the mower."

"Yeah. They're coming along pretty well. Do you want something to do?"

"I guess. What?"

"There's a pile of locust logs in the old corncrib I cut last summer to sell for pit posts. They ought to be pretty well dry by now, and the bigger ones could be split into two or more lengths. Want to take a crack at it?"

"Just like old Abe Lincoln, eh? You planning to sell them?"

"That's right. There's always a market for 'em down at the mines to shore up things to stop cave-ins. I was talking to Watson at the store the other day, and he has some ready to go. He said he'd take what I had in his pickup to make a load."

"OK, Dad. I'll give it a shot."

"Good. You know where to find the steel sledgehammer in the wagon shed. There should be three steel wedges beside it along with a wood wedge."

Reed left the workshop and found the tools. He was soon at the pile of logs. As Sam said, several were large and needed splitting. He watched Sam do it many times in the past, so he knew how to proceed.

He saw a crack at the end of one log, so he drove the first wedge in to intersect with it, being careful not to set it too deep. The crack bean to widen, and he drove in the second wedge farther down the log. By the time he drove in the third wedge even farther down, the crack widened enough that the first wedge was loose. With a tap from the sledgehammer, it came out. He repeated the process, working his way down the log, until the crack extended the full length, and the log split into two pieces.

Not bad for a rookie, Reed thought.

In a little over an hour, he completed the task and stepped back to admire his work, as Sam came up.

"That looks like a job well done, Reed. I'll be able to call Watson, and we can get these out of here and get some money for them. You're entitled to some of that."

Reed smiled and nodded. His father didn't give praise regularly, so he felt honored.

Sam sat on the pile of posts and lit a cigarette. After a few minutes' silence, he said, "I've been meaning to mention something to you, Reed."

"Oh? Did I do something wrong?"

Sam chuckled. "No, nothing like that. More like a little advice." He took long drag on his cigarette. "I wanted to talk to you about the car wreck that killed Glenn Thomas and that woman. You're getting to the point that you're almost a man. Before long, you'll be making your own decisions about what to do

"You're old enough to know that when you drink alcohol, it affects how you make decisions. I didn't mention that Tip told me they found a bottle in the car when they pulled it from the creek. That could've had something to do with the accident. You heard what

Jimmie said about the woman who was with Glenn. You're old enough to figure out what was going on."

He paused. "You'll soon be faced with situations where you'll make your own decisions about things like alcohol and women. You'll have to abide by the results of those decisions, too. Just remember this...if you burn your ass, you're the one who'll have to sit on the blister. Understand?"

Reed nodded without speaking. Later, when he thought over Sam's comments, he felt proud that he was being treated as an adult.

Twenty-Two

Reed came in through the kitchen door accompanied by a cold breeze. The only one in the kitchen was Clara.

"I'm sure glad that job's over for a few weeks," Reed said.

"I don't even have to ask what your dad has you doing. I can tell by the smell you were cleaning the chicken house."

Reed grinned. "I made sure my shoes were cleaned off outside, so I wouldn't track some of that crap inside. An hour spent shoveling out chicken shit still leaves an odor on my clothes."

"It certainly did. I'd like you to hang your work jacket in the milk house. A few hours airing it in the cold should take care of the stink. Your shirt and pants are another matter. After you take them off, roll them up together and put them in the washing machine in the junk room. I'll do wash in another day or two."

"OK."

"What's your dad doing?"

"He said he would start the milking." Reed looked at the kitchen clock. "It's earlier than usual. Maybe he's hungrier than usual. What's for dinner?"

"You must've forgotten that this is the cook's night off. We're all going to the church for oyster supper."

"Yes, I did forget. That'll be OK. I'm not crazy about oyster stew, but they usually have a lot of other good stuff. Is your Missionary Society putting it on?"

"We'll be helping out. We made a lot of the baked goods. Actually, this is a fundraiser for the war memorial."

"War memorial? What's that about?"

"The idea is to honor all the men from the township who served in the military during this war. There's nothing definite on how or when it'll be done, but the early idea is that it'll be a stone monument with names carved in it."

"Kind of like a tombstone?"

"I guess you could say that, but it probably won't be in a cemetery."

"Where will it go?"

"That's something that'll be decided later."

"But the war's still going on. Why do this now?"

"It'll take time to raise enough money for this, and everyone hopes the war will be over soon. Anyway, we leave a little before six, so you need to get out of those clothes and take a bath."

"OK, Mom."

Jimmie sat in the living room, trying to be patient, as he waited for the rest of the family. For lack of anything else to do, he looked at Reed's schoolbooks stacked in a pile on the end table beside the sofa. The larger one was titled *Latin, the Language that Lives.* Looking through the geometry book, he saw all the numbers and drawings and decided he didn't like the subject.

Jimmie looked up, as Sam walked from the downstairs bathroom, which held just a commode and a sink.

"Golly, Dad, you smell really good."

"Is that so? I like it, too. It's the new Old Spice shaving lotion your mom got me for Christmas. Looks like you're ready to go. I will be, too, as soon as I get upstairs and pull on some clean clothes."

The family was soon on its way to the church. The trip in the car took only a few minutes, and soon, they turned off the main road, crossed the bridge over the railroad tracks, and proceeded down the gravel road past several homes before they approached the church.

Only a few other cars were parked beside the church, showing they were among the early arrivals.

Once inside, Sam, Marge, and the boys sat at the banquet tables.

"I'll take this cake I made back to the kitchen and see if they need any help," Clara said. "I'll be back in a few minutes."

Marge spoke to a woman near the front serving area. Sam tried to stay awake, only to be roused by a cold breeze, as someone came in from outside. He looked up and saw Frank and Ester Hoge coming in. Ester headed toward the kitchen carrying what looked like two pies.

"Might as well come over here and sit down, Frank," Sam said. "They aren't ready to start serving yet."

Frank hung up his coat and hat before joining Sam and the family.

"How are you folks this evening?" Frank asked. "Where's Clara?"

"We're in good shape. Clara's in the kitchen. She took in her cake, and I suspect she's jawin' with the other women back there."

"I see Marge over there. When does she have to go back?"

"We take her back the day before New Year's. her school starts the same day as mine, next Tuesday."

"Sam, I wanted to ask you about my car. Last week when I was in town to the wholesale place, at times the traffic moved slow or stopped a lot, and I saw my temperature gauge running hot. It didn't happen going in or coming back home. Maybe it's nothing. Do you think I've got a problem?"

"You'd better check it. If it overheats to the point where the cooling system doesn't work, you could blow the head gasket. It's a fifty-cent item, but you'll pay for a day and a half of labor. If the engine gets really hot, you could have a warped head or worse."

"Oh, shit. That sounds serious. What could cause it?"

"Any number of things—a leak in the radiator, a bum thermostat, the water pump goin' bad, or something as simple as a loose fan belt, so the water pump don't go like it should."

Sam paused. "Tell you what. I don't have much on my plate tomorrow. After I get the cows taken care of and eat breakfast, I'd be glad to come over and look at it. We could eliminate the simple things and decide if you need to take it back to town to a garage."

"I'd appreciate that. I sure don't want to blow up an engine. It's been two years since any new cars were made. I hear crooks are selling used vehicles that are nothing but junk."

The conversation was interrupted by a ringing sound from the end of the room near the kitchen. Reverend French stood there, smiling, with a spoon in one hand and a water glass in the other.

"I can see that I got everyone's attention," he said. "We're about ready to start, Folks. In just a minute, the ladies will start serving, and everyone needs a ticket from Sarah back there by the door. Before that, I'd like to offer a word of thanks for the food and fellowship we enjoy this evening. I'd also like to remind everyone what the purpose of this dinner is. Our young men are making great sacrifices to preserve our liberties, so it's important to honor them. Please bow your heads."

After the prayer, a line formed near the large serving window at the front of the kitchen, and food was dished out. The trays were large enough to accommodate tableware, bowls of oyster stew, and platters of fried chicken, mashed potatoes, and green beans. Baskets of rolls were placed on the tables.

Sam cautioned the boys to wait until the older members were served and seated before they got in line. Clara came out from the kitchen, and soon, all the Minor family was served and seated.

"It's really nice to eat someone else's cooking for a change," Clara said. "Everything tastes swell."

"The chicken's great," Jimmie said.

"You'd better eat your oyster stew before it's cold."

"OK, Mom. I like the broth, but those old oysters not so much. They're too big to swallow, and if you try to bite them, you get gritty stuff."

"Do the best you can. If you have a couple oysters left over, give them to your dad. He likes them."

The repast was quickly devoured, along with pie or cake from the dessert table. Most of the adults savored mugs of coffee and enjoyed their full stomachs.

In a quiet, almost-conspiratorial voice, Frank spoke to Sam and Clara. "I had a strange experience yesterday at the store." He paused to look around before continuing. "A fellow I never saw before came into the store just before mid-day to buy gas. I got it for him, and he paid for it and had the stamps."

"Nothing strange about that," Sam said.

He glanced around again. "After he got his gas, I expected him to continue on his way. Instead, he pulled away from the pumps and came back inside. He looked over the store a bit and then got a bottle of pop before sitting on the bench near the stove. He got a bit talkative and said he was on his way to Waynesburg and wondered if I had a lot of customers. Then he said he was getting kind of hungry and wondered if I could make him a sandwich. I couldn't, but I sold him a piece of cheese, and he got one of those moon pies.

"Mildred Hess came in to get a few things. She came up front with her list and ration book, and I got her order together. The stranger walked to the candy case and pretended to look at something. I looked up a couple times, and he craned his neck to watch what I did with the money and Mildred's ration book. A couple minutes after she left, he went out the door and drove off. I started thinking he was a federal agent of some kind."

"That's hard to say, Frank," Sam said. "It seems unlikely that the OPA would be concerned about a little country store when you consider what you read about counterfeit books and the black market, but you never know. The way you help folks with trading stamps or giving away extras they can't use is technically illegal, and people get arrested for it. It's better to be safe than sorry."

"That's what I figured."

"By the way, Clara said she had our new food rationing books, the ones that took effect the day after Christmas. Is there much change?"

"Not as far as canned goods and vegetables are concerned. There's a change in the meat rations, though. They cut that back a good bit."

"I heard about that. They're expecting meat shortages in coming months."

"That shouldn't affect the Minor clan much. You have your own meat on the farm."

"True, and we're able to store a lot in our frozen food locker in town after we butcher."

"If you have any surplus, we might like to buy some later."

"We'll have to be careful about that. Technically, that's a black-market transaction, and both of us would get into trouble. Maybe we can barter something."

"Probably. It'll be nice when the war's over, and we don't have to deal with shortages and rationing."

Twenty-Three

It was time for the mid-day meal, so Jimmie and Clara sat at the kitchen table.

"I'm kind of hungry, Mom. Where are Dad and Reed?"

"I sent Reed to find your father a couple minutes ago. He's probably at the workshop, so it won't be long."

"OK. What do we have to eat?"

"I opened a big jar of vegetable soup, and it's heating in that pot on the stove. That ought to go down good on a cold winter day like this."

"Sounds good."

Marge walked into the room. At the same time, the kitchen door opened, and Sam and Reed entered, bringing a gust of cold winter air. They looked down at their boots and seemed satisfied there was no accumulation of mud before they walked to the chairs at the other side of the kitchen to sit down and remove their outer wear. Clara went to the stove and began ladling soup into bowls. Without a need for spoken directions, the family members sat and began their meal.

"You've been gone all morning, Sam," Clara said. "What did you get accomplished?"

"Reed found me in the workshop I finished those maple-syrup spouts and the last of the pitman bars for the mowing machine. Earlier, I went to the store."

"The store?" Marge asked. "It's not like you to waste time with the loafers who spend half the day there doing nothing."

Sam grinned. "I made good use of my time. Last night at the church dinner, I spoke to Frank. He was concerned about his car overheating sometimes when he's in town. I offered to take a look and see if it was something minor I could fix."

"What was the verdict?" Clara asked.

"As soon as I started the engine and looked under the hood, I saw the problem. The fan belt was loose. It wasn't cracked or cut, so all we had to do was tighten it."

"Did he pay you something for fixing it?"

"He offered, but I can't take money for a little thing like that. From start to finish took five minutes."

"Huh. Everyone around here knows you're the guy to hood-wink into getting something for nothing."

An annoyed look came to Sam's face. He seemed ready to reply, then he stopped, looked down, and concentrated on his soup.

"There's such a thing as being neighborly," Marge said.

"And there's such a thing as always being taken advantage of," Clara said.

There was no conversation for a few minutes. Abruptly, the silence was broken by the ringing phone.

"Want me to answer it, Mom?" Reed asked.

"Yes, would you please? It'll save me some steps."

A few moments later, Reed returned to the kitchen. "It's for you, Dad. It's Watson."

"I know what that's about. I talked to him at the store this morning. He said he'd call before he stopped by with his pickup to get the pit posts."

Several minutes later, they ate canned peaches for dessert.

"These are really good, Clara," Marge said. "They're so much better than what you get from those metal cans in the stores."

"I'd glad you like them. I have only a few quarts left in the cellar."

Marge said, "I've really enjoyed my holiday, and I hate leaving here on Sunday. I've been thinking I'd like to treat all of you to a movie tonight. Any reason we can't do that?"

"I can't think of any," Clara said. "That would be really nice. Can we do that, Sam?"

"I don't see any reason why not. The week off from school put me ahead on my gasoline allotment. Come Tuesday, it'll be a new month."

"Is there anything good playing?" Clara asked.

"I looked at the newspaper," Marge said. "*Sweet Rosie O'Grady* with Betty Grable is at the State. It played in Pittsburgh last summer, but I couldn't get in to see it. It's supposed to be good."

"Do you know what it's about or what the storyline is?"

"It's a musical with singing and dancing. I don't know about plot, but I'm pretty sure it's not a heavy drama. Oh, yes. It's in Technicolor."

"Sounds good to me," Clara said. "Everyone OK with that?"

"I thought *Marine Raiders* with Pat O'Brien was playing at the Washington," Reed said.

"I'm afraid that must've moved on," Marge said. "I checked the listing, and there was some cowboy thing playing there."

"I guess we're all set," Sam said. "We need to get the milking done a bit early, so we can get there by show time."

Sam and Reed went to the barn, while Clara and Marge relaxed in the kitchen before starting supper. Their solitude was interrupted by the ringing phone.

"Who in the world can that be?" Clara asked. "I guess I won't know unless I answer the phone."

She walked from the kitchen, and Marge picked up the newspaper on the table to check the society pages, wondering if there were any articles about someone she knew. Several minutes passed, and she was surprised at the length of Clara's call. She heard Clara's voice faintly but couldn't make out the words.

Finally, she heard Clara say, "Good-bye." A few moments later, Clara returned to the kitchen looking crestfallen.

"That's not a happy expression," Marge said. "Bad news?"

"I'm afraid so. That was Grace, my younger sister. That poor girl, just when it seems like she has a bit of good luck, things fall apart. Her husband's sick and in the hospital. He had appendicitis, and it burst, so now he's got peritonitis, which is very serious. She said they hope to use a new drug called penicillin, but they have trouble getting it even at the hospital."

"I've heard of penicillin. Which hospital is he at?"

"It's a Morgantown, across the line down in West Virginia. It's the closest to where they live. She was lucky their minister has a sister who lives in Morgantown, and that's where she's been staying. The two girls are with Larry's sister."

"What's the outlook?"

"Grace said the doctors were hopeful, but there should be a change one way or the other in the next two or three days."

"Will you go to visit?"

"We talked about it, but she said there isn't much I could do, so it's better to wait until we know if she'll be at the hospital or back home. She promised to call again when she knew something."

"Given this turn of events, should we cancel our trip to the movies this evening?"

"There's no point in that. We can use a little diversion."

Twenty-Four

It was midmorning, and Gayle was up only long enough to make coffee and enjoy her second cup. Sundays were her day of rest. She sat in the living room in her pajamas and a dressing gown. Standing up from the easy chair, she walked to the front window facing the street.

Not much to see, she thought. *Just another overcast, gloomy winter day. The only activity is a few dead leaves blowing around on the street. There's no point wishing the winter will be over, with at least two months before we see any signs of spring. Wanting the weather to change seems almost as futile as wanting the war to end. Both are beyond my control.*

She looked up the street in the other direction and recognized Connie, the young woman who occupied the other half of the small duplex, coming down the sidewalk. Gayle glanced at the wall clock.

It's ten-thirty. She's coming back from church. Seems to me the Catholics have two or three services. I don't think she ever misses. Church seems important to her. Her parents are gone, and her twin brother in the Air Force is her only close relative. She probably feels that being devout will enhance her prayers for his safety. I hope it's true.

Gayle watched her come up the front steps and heard the door close. She was about to return to her chair when she saw a young man on a bicycle come slowly down the street, looking at the houses. He wore a uniform and had a satchel over his shoulder secured by a strap. He passed by, then returned and stopped in front of Gayle's house. Leaning the bicycle against a tree, he looked at the papers he retrieved from his satchel, nodded, and walked toward the house.

Oh, dear God! Gayle thought. *It's Western Union! Oh, no, not a telegram from the War Department! Please, God, no, not Rex!*

She heard steps on the porch, then the doorbell rang.

It's not my doorbell, she thought. *Oh, Lord. It's Connie's.*

There were a few muffled words, then the sound of footsteps, as the messenger hurried away. Gayle heard the other door close, then a sorrowful wail.

I'd better dress and get over there. Maybe I can do something to help.

Sam settled into the easy chair in the living room and was quickly lost in thought. *I've got a full belly, and just like the old dog after he eats, I'm ready to crawl off somewhere for a nap. I guess that was the last of the Christmas leftovers. I always look forward to carcass soup from the turkey bones.*

Sounds like they're busy in the kitchen. They won't miss me for a little while, if I take a snooze.

He closed his eyes. A few moments later, he was far away.

The troop walked in two columns along the roadway.

At least it's not so cold this morning, Sam thought, *moving along helps keep a person warm. Too bad we won't get any sun today. That sure would help, but at least the clouds are high, and the Air Force boys are giving them hell.*

"Listen to the explosions just over the ridge," Tom said. "Must be from the flight of P-51s that went over a few minutes ago. That's OK by me. The more they take care of, the fewer we have to contend with."

The march continued. Soon, they reached some abandoned buildings, where the sergeant called a halt. Sam and Tom leaned into a doorway and lit cigarettes.

"Looks like a village," Tom said. "Most of these look like homes, except for the one on the other side. Maybe that was a store. Wonder where the people went?"

"Hard to say," Sam replied. "With all the fighting' through here the last couple weeks, they were smart to get the hell out."

They left the village behind and later found some bombed, smoking vehicles—two trucks and one of the new big German tanks. Several bodies were strewn about, along with miscellaneous equipment. The sergeant called another halt, and the troops looked for souvenirs.

Sam went through a small rucksack containing some hard, black bread, a cake of soap, cigarettes, and a wallet with several family pictures and official-looking papers. He found an almost-secret compartment in the wallet and took out something wrapped in tissue paper.

It was a picture of a young woman who looked like she wore a cheerleader's outfit. The letters on her sweater were *SGHS*. He wondered what they stood for.

What the hell? he thought in surprise. *A Wisconsin driver's license? I heard some German immigrants came over twenty or more years ago and went back to fight for their fatherland. I suppose he's one of those poor devils laying around here. If his folks still live in Milwaukee, they won't be putting up a gold star in their window.*

Reed came in through the front door. The sound of it closing woke Sam.

Another one of those screwy dreams, he thought. *Time I was up, anyway. I suppose we're leaving soon.*

Sam got up and walked into the kitchen. "Looks like you have everything cleaned up from dinner. I guess we're about ready to get started."

"Yes, I think so," Clara said. "If your suitcase is packed, Marge, Reed can bring it down from upstairs for you."

"That would be a help," Marge replied. "It's all ready to go."

A few minutes later, the family gathered in the living room and put on outer wear for the trip. At his father's suggestion, Reed had already started the car to let the engine warm up.

"Are you boys sure you'll be all right by yourselves this afternoon?" Clara asked. "There's plenty of room in the car, and I'm sure your Aunt Gayle would like to see you."

"No, that's OK," Reed said. "Bill will stop by soon, and we'll head down to Big Creek for some skating."

Some fun it would be at her apartment, Reed thought. *We'd be cooped up in that little living room, listening to the boring talk from the three of them while they puff on cigarettes.*

"Won't that be dangerous to skate down there, Sam?" Clara asked.

"It should be fine, Clara. The temperature hasn't been above freezing for the last four days. There should be several inches of ice."

"What about you, Jimmie?"

"I'll start that Red Randall book I got for Christmas."

"Well, all right. You both know the rules, so behave yourselves."

Soon, the car with the three adults pulled up in front of a small double house.

"Things look pretty quiet in this neighborhood," Sam observed. "There's nobody out for a walk. People must be taking it easy and resting before the work week starts on Tuesday."

They got out and walked up to the porch. As they mounted the steps, the door opened, and Gayle greeted them with a smile.

"I can't say this is a nice surprise, since I knew you were coming," Gayle said. "I'll just say it's nice. I've been looking out my front window for the past hour. I don't get much company, so this is a special occasion."

Once inside, they sat and enjoyed the coffee and cookies Gayle prepared.

"Any excitement around here today?" Marge asked.

"As a matter of fact, there was." Gayle related the earlier experience with her next-door neighbor and the Western-Union messenger. She added how she went to offer sympathy and comfort to the young woman.

"It's small comfort," she finished, "but the telegram from the War Department didn't say her brother was killed, just that he was missing in action. At least she has some hope. I told her not to expect any more information soon. After I was told Ralph was missing, it was over four months before I learned he was a POW."

"Does she have other family?" Clara asked.

"No. It's just her and her brother. I never pried, but she told me their family lived a few miles north of Pittsburgh along the Allegheny River. Their parents and two younger siblings drowned in the thirty-six flood."

Gayle paused. "It was just after she came home from church that I was looking out my front window and saw the messenger boy come up the walk. Dear God, my heart was in my throat. I was afraid he had a telegram about Rex. When it turned out to be for Connie next door, I felt relieved and guilty."

"You shouldn't feel guilty," Marge said. "This damned war is stressing everyone a dozen different ways."

"Have you heard from Rex recently?" Sam asked.

"Yes. I got a V mail from him Thursday. It was only a few lines. He isn't much of a letter writer to begin with, and they blank out anything about where they are or what they're doing. The letter was dated the tenth, and that was before the big battle started, so I don't really know anything."

"I suppose you have to be back at the dress shop on Tuesday?" Clara asked.

"That's right. Mr. Siegel plans for a winter clearance sale starting in a week, so there's plenty to do to prepare for that. We need to make room for the spring clothing that comes in later this month.

He said the other day we're getting several new lines for the year. It's almost as much variety as before the war. On Tuesday, it's back to the salt mines."

"I can relate to that," Marge said, "but at least you're dealing with adults. I'll be stuck in classrooms full of kids, where only one or two out of thirty are interested in learning."

Her remarks triggered several thoughts for Sam. *It's a pity she seems to detest teaching so much. Maybe that's because she doesn't enjoy being around young people. She probably should've chosen another line of work, but there aren't many choices for women. Teaching and nursing are about it. Nursing's no bed of roses, either. It's hard work, long hours, and there's the temptation to take dope to get through.*

I enjoy being around young people and helping them learn. Maybe I get too close, sometimes. Two or three of the senior boys in my physics class last year were drafted or enlisted right after graduation. Now they're in the middle of the war somewhere. I heard that little Janson fellow who graduated in '43 is a bombardier somewhere in the European Theater. I hate to see them going in harm's way. They're not much more than kids.

Sam's reverie was interrupted by laughter. "What's so funny? I wasn't paying attention to what you were talking about."

Clara smiled. "I was telling them about the time last summer Jimmie thought he could learn how to be a tightrope walker in the backyard. He got the idea they tied their feet to the wire and slid along. It didn't work too well when he tied himself to the clothesline you put up for me. I had to help get him down when I heard him yelling."

"That must've been quite a spectacle. I'm glad I missed it. I hate to be the one to break up a party, but the afternoon's getting along. We need to get Marge to the streetcar station."

"I'm glad you were able to stop," Gayle said. "I wish you could stay longer, but I know you have to meet the schedule. Let me get your coats."

A few minutes later, the three were in the car, driving toward downtown.

"What time does your streetcar leave, Marge?" Sam asked.

"Four-fifteen."

"It looks like we'll get there with plenty of time to spare."

"I would've liked spending more time visiting with Gayle, but the next streetcar going into the Pittsburgh area on Sunday doesn't leave until a quarter before six. By the time I got back, caught a bus, and got to my place, it would be ten o'clock or later until I got to bed. That would make for a long day."

"I can see that," Clara said. "At least you'd have a day to rest before school starts on Tuesday."

"Not as much as you might think. I'll be busy. You'd be amazed at the amount of soot and grit that has seeped in over the weekend. Those steel mills are running around the clock, seven days a week, and they put a lot of stuff into the air. Sometimes, I think most of it ends up in my apartment.

"What about you, Sam?" Marge asked. "I hope you'll take it easy on New Year's Day."

"Somewhat," he replied. "Of course, the cows have to be milked, and I'll have to throw hay at the beef cattle. Beyond that, the only thing I have in mind is listening to the Rose Bowl game. I'll probably find that on the radio somewhere."

"Rose Bowl? I'm not much of a football fan, but I thought they discontinued that once the war started."

"Oh, no. They thought about canceling it in '42, because of the threat of a Japanese attack on the west coast in the aftermath of Pearl Harbor, so they moved it to North Carolina, to Duke University. Every year since, they've held it back in California."

"Who's playing this year?"

"Southern California and Tennessee."

"Do you think your alma mater will ever make it back?"

"Oh, no. W and J was the last small college to make it, and it's only about the big colleges and universities now. Their glory time was in the early twenties, a couple years before I was there."

"Speaking of the radio, did you hear any news today?"

"I suppose you mean war news. Generally, it sounds pretty good. The Air Force is continuing to beat up the German positions and supply lines. The land forces are consolidating the recent gains, and the correspondents are guessing that Patton's Third Army is about to launch a major offensive. Apparently, the idea is to pinch off the bulge of the German forces that pushed into Belgium and cut off their retreat."

"Would that be the end of it?"

"I'm afraid not. They don't seem to know when they're licked. There was mention of a Berlin radio broadcast by Hitler. He said the end of the war wouldn't come until 1946, unless by a German victory, because Germany would never capitulate."

"That's very discouraging. Is it true?"

"I don't have a crystal ball, but they're being hammered from all sides. At some point, they'll run out of manpower and resources. Lord knows, it's been a drain on our manpower. I read in the newspaper recently that something over 850,000 men have been inducted from the start of Selective Service through this past November just from Pennsylvania alone."

Soon, they were near the streetcar station.

"Looks like we're in luck," Sam said. "There are two parking spots in front."

As Clara and Sam drove home after their visit, they were lost in thought for the first few miles. The roadway was bare, though the adjoining fields were snow-covered.

"If we don't get any more snow," Clara said, "you shouldn't have any trouble driving to school on Tuesday."

"I hope you're right. It's not much fun wrestling with the chains first thing in the morning."

As they drove, the clouds broke up, revealing patches of blue sky. Fast-moving clouds scudded by, and the sun reflected on the snow cover to brighten the landscape.

"That sure is bright, almost enough to hurt my eyes," Clara said. "Maybe I shouldn't complain. Perhaps it's a positive sign. The New Year begins tomorrow, so maybe it'll be a good one."

"Good would be nice, though it's hard to be hopeful. Recently, I've been thinking that life is just one kick in the ass after another."

"Could be there's a silver lining somewhere. Remember what your mom always said?"

"You mean that bit about, 'It's always darkest before the dawn'? My mother was one of the kindest, sweetest people who ever walked the earth. In some respects, though, she was gullible and a bit naïve when it came to looking at things realistically. Remember a couple of years after the crash, when for all practical purposes, Dad was broke so bad we almost lost the farm? She never had a frown on her face. Something in her makeup refused to acknowledge anything negative.

"I haven't told you," he said after a moment, "but I've been having a bunch of weird dreams that don't make much sense. They've kinda put my mind in a twist."

Clara frowned. "What kind of dreams?"

"They take place in the military, in war zones."

"Who's in them? Do you recognize anyone?"

"I'm in them. In one, I was about to be shot by Germans just as I woke up. In others, people were being killed. They aren't pleasant dreams."

"That does seem strange, since you were never in the military."

"I wonder if I have one of those subconscious guilt complexes."

"About what?"

"There are plenty of men older than me serving. Maybe I should have enlisted."

"Oh, for God's sake! How would we have survived? The boys and I would've starved."

"Probably not. With a college education, I'd have gone into officers training, and you'd have been OK financially."

"Sam, that's the craziest thing you've come up with the entire time we've been married."

"I agree. It didn't happen, and it won't. I'm just trying to understand why I've been having those strange dreams. They might be affecting my outlook."

Sam sighed. "I don't know what's wrong with me. It's always been my nature to look on the bright side of things. Over the last few weeks, I've been worn down and find myself dwelling on the negatives. The war news from Europe has been good the last couple of days, but then we visit Gayle and hear about that poor woman next door who lost her only close relative. I suspect in the next few days, there'll be hundreds, maybe thousands, of folks getting similar telegrams. What an awful price to pay just to put a gold star in the window."

"I have to admit I've had some of those feelings, too. Maybe we're dwelling too much on the day-to-day and week-to-week things."

"That's hard to ignore with all that's going on and what we face."

"True, but remember that most of them, like the progress of the war, rationing, and the other restrictions, are items over which we have no control."

"OK. What's your point?"

"Maybe we should focus on things a little further ahead that we might be able to influence or control. For example, we have two bright, young boys at home who should be given a chance at a college education. How will we make that happen? The mortgage on the farm is with a private individual who won't live forever, and all we've ever paid is the interest. We need to plan how to pay that off. Finally, though we're only in our forties, we need to think about our later years. None of those have easy answers, but they should have a positive focus."

"I can't argue with any of that, but it's hard not to be skeptical."

"After today, we'll have this dark December behind us. Soon we'll see the days getting longer. Maybe that'll give us incentive to look forward in a positive way."

As they reached home, Sam pulled into the lane and up into the garage. He and Clara walked the short distance across the yard onto the porch. As Clara opened the front door into the living room, the phone rang. Without removing her coat, she walked the few steps into the office area and answered.

"Hello? Oh, hello, Grace. What's the news?" She paused. "Oh, no! Oh, Grace, Honey, that can't be." She paused again. "Oh, Sweetheart, that's so unfair. You have to get hold of yourself and be strong for yourself and the girls. Yes, I will. We'll be down by noon. I'll stay as long as necessary to help you through this.

Clara hung up and walked into the living room. She sat on the sofa, still wearing her coat, and looked at Sam.

"I guess you heard enough to figure out that Larry died," she said sadly. "Oh, Grace. That poor girl. She'll have a tough row to hoe. It makes our problems seem pretty insignificant."

"And all this time," Clara said, "I worried he might be drafted. Damn the luck."

Jack Dunn is a native of south western Pennsylvania. He holds undergraduate and graduate degrees from Penn State University. His professional life was at the executive management level in the field of planning and community development. He retired from the position of Director of the York County Planning Commission after serving in that position for thirty-five years in 2000. He is a past President of the Pennsylvania Planning Association. His interests include environmental and energy issues, genealogy and history. His son Bradley lives in York, Pennsylvania. Jack resides in north eastern Pennsylvania with his partner, Naomi Meyer.